Rel X
Relling, William.
Sweet poison : a Jack
    Donne mystery $ 22.95

SWEET POISON

Also by William Relling Jr.

Deadly Vintage

SWEET POISON

A JACK DONNE MYSTERY

William Relling Jr.

WALKER AND COMPANY

New York

First published in the United States of America in 1998 by
Walker Publishing Company, Inc.

Published simultaneously in Canada by Thomas Allen & Son
Canada, Limited, Markham, Ontario

Library of Congress Cataloging-in-Publication Data
Relling, William.
Sweet poison : a Jack Donne mystery / William Relling Jr.
p. cm.
ISBN 0-8027-3316-6
I. Title.
PS3568.E554S94 1998
813'.54—dc21 97-47720
CIP

Series design by Mauna Eichner

Printed in the United States of America
2 4 6 8 10 9 7 5 3 1

To the memory of Rex Stout

I owe particular thanks to three people, without whom *Sweet Poison* would not exist: my excellent friend Nathan Walpow, the *real* Peter Taylor of Santa Ynez, and the *real* Dan Gainey of Gainey Vineyards, likewise of Santa Ynez. Here's a toast to your health, happiness, and success, guys.

—WRjr

Bacchus, that first from out the purple grape
Crush'd the sweet poison of misused wine.

John Milton

Only the man who knows too little knows too much.

Nero Wolfe

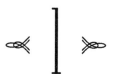

O f the three of us getting into the taxicab a little after nine o'clock in the morning, I was the second to spot the runaway Econoline van careening our way. The first to see it was Carla Lubow. She was sitting in the cab's backseat when she happened to turn around and look over her shoulder.

I noticed it only after Carla screamed.

Her scream made me glance up from trying to wedge our employer, Mr. Augustus Poole, into the seat beside her. I looked over at Carla, then turned toward where she was pointing.

The cab was idling in front of Mr. Poole's residence, double-parked on Jones Street, a couple of houses up from the base of Russian Hill. By the time I spotted the van, it was closing fast. I could tell it was a runaway by the way it weaved from side to side, doing none too good a job of staying on the proper side of the yellow line. It scraped the vehicles parked on either side of Jones Street, making shrill skreeks of metal on metal. I also could tell it was a runaway because there was no driver behind the wheel. Nobody in the van at all, as far as I could tell.

What I did was strictly reflex. I'd been trying to shimmy Mr.

Poole's substantial bulk through what was for him a too-narrow opening. Registering the van's imminent arrival, I grabbed the fat man by the collar, planted my feet firmly, and yanked him backward with all my strength. He popped out of the cab's door like a champagne cork, and the two of us went tumbling ass-over-teakettle. We landed in a heap on the other side of the street, with me on the bottom—crushed beneath 300-odd pounds of squirming human flesh.

I didn't see what happened with the van, but as it turned out, our cabbie's reflexes were as good as my own. He spotted the runaway in his side-view mirror, shifted from park into drive, and jammed his foot on the accelerator, whipping the steering wheel at the same time. The cab shot forward and swung a wide turn into the intersection at the bottom of Jones Street. The cab's open rear door whanged against a couple of parked cars an instant before the runaway van reached the bottom of the incline. The van's front wheels made a sudden, hard lurch to the left, causing the whole thing to tip over. It skidded on its side, sliding through the intersection and raising an impressive shower of sparks before smashing, roof first, against a lamppost.

But as I said, I didn't see any of this. I heard it well enough—the crunching of metal, the shattering of glass, the screeching of brakes, the honking of horns. But I didn't see anything, because I was busy trying to crawl out from under Mr. Poole before he smothered me to death.

At last we managed to untangle ourselves and sat there on the curb, breathing heavily. He glared at me as if to say, What in God's name did you think you were doing?

I was working too hard at trying to suck air into my deflated lungs to say anything. I managed to wave a hand in the direction of the intersection, where, judging from the sound, an excited crowd was gathering. I could also hear the distant wail of an approaching police siren.

At my gesture, Poole turned toward the intersection. He studied the scene for a moment, narrowing his eyes. Then he turned back to me. Evidently he'd made up his mind what had happened, because his angry expression had become haughty and smug.

"Well, Mr. Donne?" he said.

I was still short of breath. "Well, what?"

He looked at me as if he thought he was speaking to a moron. "Now do you believe that someone is trying to kill me?"

IF I'D FELT motivated, I probably could have assured Poole that a runaway delivery van makes for a mighty unreliable murder weapon. Effective, maybe, if the vehicle happened to hit you head-on, but not nearly so easy to aim as, say, your basic Saturday night special.

And indeed attempted murder turned out not to have been the case. I'd already guessed this even before a uniformed San Francisco Police Department patrolman informed me that the van's driver had been delivering flowers to one of Poole's neighbors up the street. The driver had simply done a crappy job of parking. Not only had he forgotten to turn his wheels to the curb—which should be a capital offense in San Francisco—but he'd also not bothered to engage his emergency brake. To me it was nothing more than a textbook example of Murphy's Law. Once the van's transmission accidentally slipped into neutral, all it took was a little gravity to send the thing hurtling downhill. Toward us.

Eventually, even Poole seemed convinced there was nothing

deliberate about what had happened with the runaway van. Unless you believed—as I was beginning to—that some higher power might have it in for him. I'd been in the man's company for a fairly short time, but it wasn't hard for me to conceive that, given the personality he'd demonstrated, he'd accrued a pretty serious karmic debt over his fifty years of life. Were I one of the powers that be, I might want to run him over with a truck myself.

By the time everything had settled down enough for us to remember why we'd been getting into a taxi in the first place, we were too late to catch the 10:00 train that was to take us to Bakersfield. Poole—to nobody's surprise, especially mine—immediately threw another fit. I can't say that by now I was getting used to his tirades, but I seemed to be getting better at ignoring them.

I'd also begun to dope out the true function of Ms. Lubow, the fat man's assistant. "It's all right, Mr. Poole," she cooed. "We'll just catch the next train. It doesn't leave until one-thirty. This way we don't have to hurry so much."

Poole's face had turned as purple as a Concord grape, but just those few soothing words from her and you could see him start to reel it in. The lull didn't last long, though. Turning away from Carla, Poole spied the cabdriver—who had probably saved Carla's life, just as I'd saved Poole's. The cabbie—a short, skinny, scraggly-bearded Middle Easterner—was attempting to explain in pidgin English what had happened with the cab and the van. He was speaking to the same SFPD patrolman who'd spoken to me earlier.

Poole bellowed to the cabdriver, "You, boy! Stop right there!"

Both the cabbie and the cop—who happened to be a black man—turned around. Advancing upon them, Poole commenced berating the poor cabbie. My obese employer seemed to have forgotten that his assistant had just informed him we had better than three hours till the next train. He began demanding that the cabdriver return to his vehicle at once, so as to convey Poole, Carla, and me to the Emeryville Amtrak station without further delay. The cabdriver, the cop, and Poole commenced an angry, three-way exchange that hit peak volume about ten seconds after it began.

I'd stopped listening by then. I figured the thing to do instead was ask Carla to let me back in the house so I could phone for another cab. Walking up the steps, I asked myself for the umpteenth time how I'd managed to get talked into nursemaiding one of the most loathsome individuals it had ever been my displeasure to meet.

It was a rhetorical question, since of course I knew the answer. I was doing a favor—partly for my uncle Gerry, and partly for my friend Peter Taylor.

The series of events culminating with my saving Augustus Poole from a runaway florist's van had begun some four weeks before, a couple of Sundays following Memorial Day. According to the calendar, June 21 was still several days away, but I'd been in my own personal summer mode since the middle of May. In my business—I grow grapes and make wine for a living—summer is usually a pleasant time of year. Most of the vinicultural work has been done. The fruit needs minimal tending—keeping an eye out for weeds and pests, too much or too little sun and water, that sort of thing. But it's not at all like the fall harvest season, when things get busiest. Nor is it like winter, when the rains come and everything slows to a molasses crawl, or spring, when you have to pay close attention to getting a new vintage started.

Not much actually happens during the summer. The vines have made their growth, and the fruit is beginning to ripen, but everyone's cellars are about as idle as they get. That's one reason why summer is when winemakers open their doors to visitors who'd like to take a look around and sample whatever wares you might be marketing. A little simple PR, if you will.

Different winemakers have different rules for strangers. Some open tasting rooms, some conduct full-blown tours of their facilities, and some just hang a surly sign, "Keep Out: This Means You." We at Donne Vineyards—the business co-owned by my father, my uncle Gerry, and me—invite people to drop by on weekends during the summer. Though we don't have a regular tour, Dad and I are happy to show you around. Most tourists, though, are less interested in a behind-the-scenes look than they are in quaffing a bit of wine. That's why we devote most of our energy to operating a small tasting room, from 11:00 A.M. till 5:00 P.M., Saturdays and Sundays, May through September.

"We" being—besides myself—my father and our sole full-time employee, Jesus Fonseca. My uncle Gerry—Dad's brother—is a full partner in the business, but he has little to do with anything that involves getting sweaty or dirty. Gerry Donne is one of southern California's more highly regarded financial lawyers. He takes care of the suit-and-tie portion of Donne Vineyards, Inc., operating out of a spacious office suite in downtown Santa Barbara. His office is a forty-five-minute drive from the grape-growing and wine-manufacturing end of the family business, out in San Tomas, in the northern Santa Ynez Valley. His home is also in Santa Barbara—on the grounds of the La Cumbre Golf and Country Club—barely a hop, skip, and a jump from where he works.

That he lives rather far away from us—Dad and I share a ranch-style house that sits on the vineyard's grounds—makes it a surprise whenever Gerry drops by unannounced. That, plus his legal-beagle nature, which insists you should always call first to make sure there isn't a previous appointment ahead of you.

As it was a Sunday afternoon in June, a little past four o'clock, my uncle could be reasonably certain where he'd find us. We've set up Donne Vineyards' tasting room in the smallest of four outbuildings arranged in a U around the main house. It gets warm in the valley during the summer—the mean midday temperature from the end of June through the beginning of October regularly pushes ninety degrees, and I can attest from having lived here for much of my life that as often as not it pushes pretty hard.

This day was no exception. I'd checked an outdoor thermometer around noon and noted that it was ninety-two in the shade. Dad and I keep things dark and cool in the tasting room, the interior air-conditioned to around sixty-eight—our attempt to approximate the feel of a wine cellar. Because Donne Vineyards is somewhat isolated from the other wineries in the valley, usually by the time guests arrive they've been out in the sun for a while. They tend to be mighty hot and mighty thirsty.

This particular Sunday had been about average, in terms of visitor trade, with a couple dozen folks moseying up the long driveway to the gravel lot that fronts our house. We were pouring our most recent chardonnay release, chilled chard being popular among dry and dusty tourists, and by midafternoon we'd sold four or five cases of wine.

Our visitor traffic had slowed, as it usually did by that time of day. Dad and I were alone in the tasting room when I spotted my uncle's Cadillac Seville rolling up the drive. Dad was sitting behind the makeshift bar we set up on weekends, one hand resting on the quad cane he's used to help himself get around ever since his stroke, a few years back. I was leaning on the sill of the tasting room's only window, peering out toward the heat shimmers rising off Highway 154 a quarter of a mile away.

Hearing the crunch of tires on gravel, Dad questioned me with a look: More customers?

"It's Uncle Gerry," I said.

"Uncle Gerry?"

"Uh-huh. How come you didn't tell me he'd be stopping by?"

"I didn't know," Dad said.

I looked at him over my shoulder, surprised. "You didn't?"

Dad shook his head.

I turned back to the window. By then Gerry had braked his car, raising a small cloud of dust. He shut off the Caddy's engine, and the car shuddered for a moment, like a hippopotamus shaking itself dry after a dip in the river. The car settled, just as Gerry was emerging from the driver's side. He spotted me, smiled, and waved hello.

Typical of the men in our family, Gerry is a good-size human being. Like my dad, he's an inch shorter than my 6′ 2″— which still makes both of them taller than the average American male, though since his stroke Dad hobbles with a pronounced stoop that makes him seem shorter. Dad, who is two years younger than Gerry, is also built more like me—lean and lanky, instead of wide-bodied, like my uncle. The two of them have the same freckled, easy-to-sunburn skin I have—inherited from our Scottish ancestors—and the same shock of straight, straw-colored hair, though my father's and my uncle's turned gray some years ago. Gerry's face is fuller than either my dad's or mine, but all three of us have the same dark, deep-set eyes—making for the kind of expression my late mother often used to call "brooding."

While that may be a term you could apply at times to my own temperament, my dad and my uncle are anything but. Which isn't to say they don't have their dark sides. Dad and Gerry are as hotheaded and mulish as any Scotsmen, and they disagree with each other and anyone else on any number of issues—politics, sports, religion, you name it. But ever since combining their resources to start Donne Vineyards, they've made for a great team—Dad the visionary, Gerry the one to execute the business part of the vision. Both of them are passionate, good-humored men, and they are as close as any pair of partners, brothers, and friends can be.

Gerry, who favors neckties and custom-tailored suits when he's working, was dressed in what was for him weekend-casual attire: polo shirt, Eddie Bauer khakis, Top-Siders. As he strode to the entrance to the tasting room, I crossed to open the door.

"How's it goin', nephew?" he said, grinning as he entered.

I smiled a greeting in return, closing the door behind him to keep the cool air in and the warm air out. I followed him to the bar, where Dad was already pouring glasses of chard for the three of us. He'd taken the bottle from a cabinet behind him, instead of the small refrigerator where we keep chilled wine for strangers. We Donnes prefer our chardonnay to be cool, not cold. My father and uncle taught me long ago that the vast majority of people in this country drink their white wine too cold and their red too warm.

As I came up to join them at the bar, Dad was saying to Gerry, "You just happen to be in the neighborhood, or what? It's not like you to drop by without calling first."

"I've called half a dozen times since noon," Gerry said. "Nobody answered."

"Believe it or not, we've actually had customers," I told him.

"You two are doing the pouring?" Gerry asked. I nodded. He said, "Where's Jesus?"

"Dad gave him the day off."

Uncle Gerry lifted his glass to inhale the chard's bouquet. "You should at least check your messages once in a while. Or else bring the phone out here with you. What if it was something urgent?"

Dad snorted, dismissing the notion with an abrupt wave of

his hand. He dislikes telephones as much as I do.

"Is it?" I asked.

"Urgent?" Gerry shook his head. "Not exactly." He took a sip of wine, savored it, then looked at me. "You free for dinner, Jack?"

"Tonight?"

He nodded. "I was playing golf this morning with Peter Taylor. Just as we were coming up on the sixteenth tee, he said, 'Do you know if Jack's doing anything for dinner?' I told him I didn't, and he asked me if I could find out. If you're free, I'm supposed to bring you over." Gerry turned to my dad. "You too, Ray. Peter said you'd be welcome to come along. Though he really just wants to talk to Jack about some personal business."

"Personal business?" I asked, puzzled.

"Not wine-type business," explained Gerry. "Detective-type business."

I groaned.

A LITTLE OVER two years ago, I'd finally made myself comfortable with the notion of getting out of the law enforcement game for good and into the wine business instead. I'd held some kind of cop-related job for most of the previous two decades—starting right out of college with my hitch in the air force, where I was an MP. After that I joined the Bureau of Alcohol, Tobacco and Firearms as a special agent, attached to the Los Angeles field office and specializing in undercover activity.

Ten years later, while attempting to pass myself off as a money launderer to a couple of gunrunning con men, I had my cover broken. Which got me a .22 slug in the kneecap for my trouble—followed by a couple of months' worth of physical therapy and an offer from the Bureau of a permanent desk job, since

I was no longer deemed fit for fieldwork. What I did instead, being at core an active sort of individual, was opt for early retirement and a disability pension. I wasn't quite ready to stop going after criminals, so I moved to Santa Barbara and hung out a shingle: J. B. DONNE— PRIVATE INVESTIGATIONS.

As it turned out, I hunted down few actual crooks. Mostly what I did was hustle around for a bunch of lawyers—among them Uncle Gerry—none of whom really wanted me to do anything more daring than run background checks and chase paper trails. Being a private eye ended up a lot more tedious and unglamorous a job than I'd expected. *Spenser for Hire* it wasn't.

Then, when Dad suffered his stroke, it occurred to me that it might be time to get out of the crime-fighting business—however peripherally I was involved in it by then—and into the family business instead, which my father and my uncle had been after me to do for some time anyway. I soon discovered that not only did I have an aptitude for winemaking but I also enjoyed the work, taking to it like the proverbial fish to the proverbial wet stuff. Before long I wasn't even looking back on—much less missing—my days as one of the good guys going after the bad guys.

Then, this past April, I found myself involved in unraveling a wine-counterfeiting scam aimed at the Santa Ynez Valley's largest and richest winemaking operation, owned and operated by a guy named Ozzie Cole. Part of the scam concerned Ozzie's being framed for the murder of his own father. I ended up briefly becoming a PI again—clearing Ozzie of murder charges, unmasking the real killer, and causing the scam to blow up in the faces of the perpetrators. I played a key role, not only in seeing that some bad people got put behind bars where they belonged but in effecting the deaths of four human beings. Some indirectly, some less so.

And, overall, I did not enjoy the experience.

Part of that had to do with working on behalf of Ozzie Cole, Ozzie being a rather unpleasant individual. Part of it had to do with some feelings of guilt I'd developed over having been mixed up in four deaths, feelings that in at least one instance—the only one I was directly responsible for—were somewhat irrational. And part of it had to do with a realization that, after my business with Ozzie Cole was concluded, I really had put all that cops-and-robbers crap behind me. I just wanted to make wine.

I also didn't enjoy the sort of small-scale notoriety and local celebrity that seemed to come with my having been in the thick of the Ozzie Cole case. Fortunately, by mid-June, all of that finally seemed to be blowing over.

Or so I thought.

AT FIVE O'CLOCK we closed the tasting room and went into the house. While Dad headed back to his bathroom to take a shower, Gerry and I went into the den I use for my office. I went to the phone on my desk and played back the messages Dad and I'd got while we were pouring samples. It turned out my uncle had been exaggerating. He'd called only three times.

Reaching for my Rolodex, I looked up Peter Taylor's number. He answered on the second ring. "Rancho Calzada. Peter speaking."

"Peter, it's Jack Donne."

"Hey, Jack, I'm glad you called. I take it you talked to your uncle?"

"He's standing right here."

"So?" Peter asked. "You free for dinner tonight?"

"As it happens, we are. But what's this about you wanting to talk over some detective business with me?"

A pause. "I didn't tell Gerry what this is about 'cause I'd rather lay it out for you in person. All at once."

There was a curious emotional quality to the tone of his voice—not apprehension, exactly, but a sort of reluctance. "It's not something you can talk to me about over the phone?" I asked.

"No, no—nothing like that." He sighed. "It'll just be better if I tell you face-to-face."

I considered for a moment. Then: "What time do you want us?"

"Seven o'clock all right?"

"We'll be there," I told him.

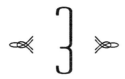

P eter Taylor was saying to me, "What do you know about NAMES?"

There were six of us seated around one of a dozen or so small, circular tables in the banquet room of El Rancho de las Calzadas: my dad, my uncle, Peter, his mother, Joyce, his father, Ted, and me. It was a little after 8:00 P.M. We'd finished dinner—a charbroiled salmon steak for each of us, with steamed vegetables on the side and fresh-baked sourdough bread—and were starting on dessert, Ted having broken out a bottle of '63 Dow's from his personal stash.

The Taylors are a handsome family. Joyce and Ted are both in their sixties, though they could pass for a decade younger. Peter looks like a combination of his parents: a slender man, four or five inches shorter than I am, with green eyes and thinning brown hair. His skin and his father's have the perpetual ruddiness of men who spend a lot of time in the hot sun but don't tan particularly well.

Along with the port, Joyce had dished up a bowl of strawberries and whipped cream for all of us. As I forked a berry into my mouth, I asked Peter, "Whose names?"

He shook his head. "Not 'names' as in, 'Hi, my name's Jack Donne.' I mean the organization NAMES. N-A-M-E-S."

Uncle Gerry said, "The North American Epicurean Society."

"Oh," I said. "Those NAMES."

"What do you know about 'em?" Peter asked.

I considered for a moment. "Kind of a stuck-up group, aren't they? Mostly upscale restaurateurs, chefs, food critics, wine mavens, that sort of thing? Membership by invitation only?" I paused. "How'm I doing so far?"

"Not bad," said Ted, lifting his glass in a toast. I bowed, acknowledging the gesture.

Dad grunted. "Snooty bastards."

Uncle Gerry said to the Taylors, "Ray's just mad because he's never been asked to join."

"Who'd want to join?" said Dad.

"Actually," Ted said, "I would. That's why we're hosting their banquet next month."

I let out a low whistle. "Rancho Calzada is hosting the NAMES banquet? I'm impressed."

"It took some doing," Peter admitted. "Dad's been trying to cadge a membership for years. He finally got somebody in the group to sponsor him. You know Terry Elliott, don't you?"

"Very well," said Gerry. Elliott, like Peter, was another of my uncle's golfing buddies.

Ted said, "Terry's been a Rancho Calzada customer for a long time, and like Peter says, he's the one who's sponsoring me. But getting sponsored is only the first hurdle. I haven't been officially invited to join yet. That's why we're hosting the banquet."

"What is it?" I asked jokingly. "Some kind of frat house initiation? You serve 'em one lousy meal and you're out the door?"

Joyce looked a bit chagrined. "You're not far wrong, Jack."

Dad snorted. "You're kidding. If your meal doesn't pass muster, they won't let you in their club?" He shook his head, disgusted, then repeated, "Snooty bastards."

"So what do you need me for?" I asked Ted.

He took a deep breath. "I know you're out of the private eye business, but I really could use a favor. Not that it won't be anything less than a professional arrangement. You'll be well paid, I promise you."

I could feel the back of my neck prickling. "What's the favor?"

"Do you know how these annual NAMES shindigs operate?" he asked. "What the procedure is, I mean?"

I shook my head.

"They limit their entire membership to just fifty-seven people, and they only take on a new member when an old one either gets booted out or resigns—which nobody's ever done—or dies."

"Why fifty-seven people?" I asked.

"It was the founders' idea of a little joke," said Peter. "You know—making fun of Heinz 57?"

"Very amusing."

Ted shrugged. "Anyway, since last year's banquet, they've had two openings."

"Deaths?" I asked.

He nodded. "But it's not what you're thinking. We're not asking you to look into a couple of murders or anything like that. Both members died of natural causes—one of 'em was a wine importer from Toronto, and the other was an editor from *Bon Apetit*, and they were both older than God." He paused. "I'm supposed to ask you, on behalf of NAMES, if you might be persuaded into being hired on as a bodyguard."

"Come again?"

He drummed his fingers on the table and looked as if he was

having a hard time deciding how to say what he wanted to say. "Every year at the banquet, the society has a guest speaker to give—I guess you'd call it an after-dinner address. It's usually somebody who's not a member, but who's nevertheless got a solid reputation among gourmets and wine snobs and such. Last year, for example, it was Cesare Giaccone from the Ristorante dei Cacciatori in Piedmont."

"Italy," explained Uncle Gerry.

"I didn't think he was talking about North Carolina." I turned back to Ted. "Go on."

"Most of the time the speakers are foreign," he continued, "although occasionally they'll have somebody like Paul Prud-homme or Robert Parker Jr. You know—a North American who isn't part of the group but still is highly enough regarded to make it okay for them to come. It's actually quite an honor to be invited. You get all your travel and expenses paid for, you get treated to a pretty fantastic meal, and the society lays a nice speaker's fee on you to boot."

"How much of a fee?" asked Dad.

"Five thousand dollars."

I whistled again. "Not bad."

Peter said, "But now we come to this year's speaker—who isn't remotely interested in doing it for the money." He looked at me pointedly. "I want you to know up front that my dad didn't have anything to do with picking him. The society puts together a committee of four or five people, and they make a recommendation. Then the whole membership gets to vote yea or nay." He paused. "Anyway, that's who we need a bodyguard for. Our 'guest.' "

Peter couldn't disguise an expression of displeasure. I asked, "Who is it?"

Ted hesitated for a moment, then said, "Augustus Poole."

My mouth fell open—and so did Dad's and Uncle Gerry's. A moment later a tiny lightbulb blinked on over my head. "Wait a minute. Are you serious? You're asking me if I'll be Augustus Poole's bodyguard?"

"I'm afraid so," said Ted.

THERE WERE DETAILS—such as who Augustus Poole was and what he did for a living—that no one had to fill me in on. Anybody in the food or beverage business would have recognized Poole's name. If he wasn't the single most influential critic in this part of the country, he was awfully close.

The most influential—and also the most obnoxious.

At that point, I'd yet to meet him. Neither was I that up on his early career. I'd been informed by a couple of people that he started as a reporter on some paper in Boston—the *Globe* presumably, though it could just as easily have been the *Back Bay Mainline* for all I knew. In typical newspaperman fashion, he moved from desk to desk, until he found himself occupying the post of restaurant critic. Eventually he parlayed that into a job in New York City, which is a mecca for food and wine writers who are as long on pontification as Augustus Poole. After building up a power base there, he relocated to the San Francisco Bay Area five or six years ago, setting himself up as a West Coast version of Gael Greene.

In California, a thumbs-up or -down from Poole—especially where a new restaurant or winery was concerned—could make the difference between whether your business flourished or withered. I know, because Donne Vineyards had been gored by him in his self-published, widely circulated, bimonthly food-and-beverage newsletter *Pooled Knowledge* on a couple of occasions. We'd been praised occasionally as well—our overall batting average was somewhere around .500—so we hadn't been nearly as ill-used as others. Still, I was aware of the man's reputation for haughtiness, condescension, and sheer gall. He could make the nastiest of critics look like Mother Teresa.

And he was going to be NAMES' guest of honor. Oh boy.

Dad asked Ted, "What's he need a bodyguard for?"

Uncle Gerry chuckled. "Are you kidding? I can think of a dozen people just off the top of my head who'd be happy to kill him."

Ted said, "All I know is, Poole's agreed to speak provided NAMES will meet three conditions. First, that he be allowed to bring along his assistant, who apparently travels with him everyplace he goes. Second, that in lieu of a cash fee he be presented a gift from the cellar of one of the society's members." He looked to my uncle. "Terry Elliott's, in fact. One of his sauternes."

Uncle Gerry raised an eyebrow, knowing as I did that his friend Terry had probably the finest personal collection of vintage dessert wines in California. "Which one?" Gerry asked.

"A '47 Chateau d'Yquem."

I whistled for the third time that evening. "Wow."

"And Terry went along with that?" my uncle asked.

Ted nodded. "Once the society agreed to compensate him. He told me he didn't mind because he still has one bottle left."

"What's the third condition?" asked Dad.

Ted sighed. "That NAMES provide him with a bodyguard. At the society's expense." He looked to me. "Whatever your usual rate is—or, I guess I should say, used to be, the society'll pick up the tab."

"You still didn't answer my dad's question," I said. "What's Poole need with a bodyguard?"

Ted shrugged. "He wouldn't tell us. He just said he had to have one, or else he wouldn't come out of his house, much less all the way down here to Santa Ynez." He paused. "I've already spoken to Poole about you, Jack."

I felt a little affronted. "Without checking with me first?"

"I apologize, but I'm kind of under the gun here. The society is really putting on the pressure to have Poole come and speak, and you were the only person I could think of off the top of my head who might be qualified to keep an eye on him."

Peter took over for his father. "He had no idea of your background, though he knew your name, of course. When Dad told him how you'd been with BATF and had even run your own detective agency for a while, Poole said it sounded like you'd be 'acceptable.' "

The table lapsed into silence for a time, until I realized that all eyes were on me. "Listen, Ted," I said finally. "I wish I could help you out. But you said it yourself. I'm not in the private eye business anymore."

Peter protested, "But what about Ozzie Cole—"

I held up a hand. "I'd really rather not repeat that experience, if it's all right with you."

All three of the Taylors looked crestfallen. "I see," said Ted. He sighed again.

Then Joyce asked, "Jack, couldn't you at least meet the man before you made up your mind once and for all?"

"Meet him where?"

"In San Francisco? Where he lives."

"San Francisco?"

Ted said, "He told me he'd be interested in interviewing you face-to-face. Just to assure himself you're the right man for the job." A pause. "The society will be happy to pick up the cost of your trip."

"A trip to San Francisco?"

Ted nodded. "That, plus your fee, plus a seat at the NAMES

banquet. Which for the past sixty years has been a members-only invitation."

I was just about to decline once more when a little voice from somewhere in the back of my mind whispered to me, San Francisco's nice. Besides, I could always say no later.

"How soon would I have to go?" I asked.

"As soon as possible," replied Ted. "The banquet's only four weeks away."

I looked to my dad.

"It's not like we're busy," Dad said.

Uncle Gerry added, "Plus you'll only be gone, what, a couple of days at the most?"

"Not even that," said Peter. "All Poole wants to do is meet you. He'll decide then and there one way or the other. You could probably make just a day trip out of it."

My uncle was grinning. "If it were me, I'd jump at an opportunity to tell Augustus Poole to go to hell directly to his face."

Ted said quickly, "Not that that's what I'm hoping you'll do."

I chewed on the notion for a while. Then I asked Ted, "Will NAMES pay for me to fly up instead of drive?"

He smiled for the first time in what seemed like hours. "Absolutely," he said.

THAT WAS HOW—on the following Wednesday—I found myself in San Francisco. I drove to Santa Barbara, leaving my Jeep Cherokee in the airport parking lot while I hopped a United Airlines shuttle that dropped me off at SF International a little after noon.

I caught a yellow cab that took me into the city, and by one-thirty I was on the stoop of a narrow three-story house on

Jones Street, ringing Augustus Poole's bell. I was expected, having been assured by Peter Taylor that he'd made an appointment for me. I'd rung the doorbell once, then waited thirty seconds or so for an indication that somebody was going to let me in. I was reaching for the bell a second time when the door was pulled open, and there stood one of the more stunning young women it's ever been my pleasure to encounter.

She was dressed in linen slacks and low-heeled shoes and a silk blouse that was open at the throat. She was on the petite side—which isn't usually my type, though I've been known to make exceptions. She stood not quite a foot shorter than me, and she had the trim, compact, athletic build of a dancer. Her hair was the color of semisweet chocolate, falling to her shoulders and framing a heart-shaped face. In contrast to her dark hair, she had the sort of peaches-and-cream complexion you'd imagine more likely on a blond Scandinavian than somebody whose other features suggested a Mediterranean heritage. Her eyes were also blue like a Scandinavian's, but her lips were as full as a Botticelli goddess's. When she smiled, I could see that she had even, white teeth. Though the smile was nothing more than a polite, perfunctory greeting to a stranger, it was a very nice smile.

"Mr. Donne?" she inquired.

I nodded.

"I'm Carla Lubow, Mr. Poole's assistant." She held out a hand for me to shake. Her grip was dry and cool. "You're very punctual."

"I try to be."

"Mr. Poole will appreciate that. Come this way, please. He's waiting for you in the office."

She closed the front door behind me, then led me from the foyer down a hallway, toward the rear of the house. Just inside the front door, the left wall was blank. A few paces down, however, we passed an open door on the right, through which I caught a glimpse of a large and expensively appointed formal dining room. A place where any number of reputations had been made or ruined, I supposed.

We moved past the dining room and came upon a right-hand side staircase leading to the second floor. Set against the stairwell was a sort of walled-in column that rose into the ceiling alongside the steps. At the base of the column was a cubicle fronted by a pair of what looked to me to be tall pantry doors made out of some dark, attractive wood.

Carla noticed the curiosity on my face as I glanced at the doors. "Mr. Poole's private elevator," she explained.

"He can't make it up and down three whole floors under his own power?"

The look she gave me suggested that I'd be wise to keep any more smart-aleck remarks to myself. I followed her down the hallway, until we came to a closed door on our left. "Wait here, please," she said.

She opened the door and went in, pushing it closed just enough so that I couldn't peep and see what was inside. I resisted an urge to rock back and forth on my heels and whistle while I waited. I heard Carla announcing my presence, then Poole's voice inviting me in. She pulled the door open and gave me a brief nod to indicate that I was to enter.

Coming into Poole's sanctum, I did my best not to show how awed I was by the immensity of the room. No doubt there were thousands of people in San Francisco who lived in entire apartments smaller than Augustus Poole's office.

But the room itself was no more immense in its way than the man who occupied it. I'd never met Augustus Poole, and I'd only seen his photograph once or twice, shot from the shoulders up.

I knew that he was supposed to be a large individual. But as I made my way to the leather chair he indicated on the opposite side of his desk, it occurred to me that calling him obese would be like saying Ken Griffey Jr. does an okay job of hitting a fastball now and then.

He was sitting behind a large desk made of cherry wood, in an oversized chair that looked sturdy enough to support about a quarter of a ton. He made another gesture for me to sit down—this time somewhat impatiently. "You'll pardon me if I don't shake hands, Mr. Donne. It's nothing personal, I assure you. It's just that I dislike being touched."

I shrugged. "Just so long as it's nothing personal."

He motioned Carla to another desk smaller than his own—hers, I assumed—against the wall over my left shoulder. As she and I took our seats, Poole said to me, "May I offer you something to drink? A glass of wine, perhaps?"

"No, thanks."

"Then let's get down to business, shall we? The Taylors have apprised me of your bona fides as a private investigator, though I also took the liberty of doing some checking on my own. You left the Treasury Department shortly after being wounded in the line of duty, is that so?"

I nodded.

"And after that, for a brief time you operated your own detective agency in Santa Ynez?"

"Santa Barbara."

"Why did you give up the detective business?"

"Mostly on account of my father. He was operating Donne Vineyards pretty much all by himself, until one day he had a stroke. It looked like he was going to be laid up for a while, and somebody needed to keep an eye on the family business. In exchange for his making me a partner, I took down my private eye shingle. I've been working at the winery ever since."

As I was speaking, he filled his cheeks with air that he blew out in soft, silent puffs. "Do you miss it?" he asked.

"Do I miss what?"

"Being a private eye?"

"Not a bit. I'm very happy doing what I do now."

"I see." He frowned. "You know why I wanted to see you, don't you?"

"You want to hire a bodyguard. So you can go to the NAMES banquet."

"Do you know why I need a bodyguard?"

I shook my head.

"Someone is trying to kill me."

"How do you know?"

"There've been two attempts on my life in the past month." He waved a chubby hand in a gesture of dismissal. "The details aren't important. What is important is that you believe me when I tell you that my life's in danger."

"I believe you," I said. "That's not the problem."

He looked puzzled.

I smiled. "I just don't want the job."

He looked as if I'd tossed ice water in his face. Then he turned red. Before he could say anything, I heard Carla asking from behind me, "Then why in God's name did you come all the way to San Francisco?"

I turned to her. "For two reasons. First, because I thought it would be interesting to meet Mr. Poole—which it is, believe me. And second, because of who he is, I thought it'd only be courteous of me to turn him down in person. That's all."

I stood up, turning back to Poole. He was still regarding me, red-faced and wide-eyed. "I've enjoyed meeting you, Mr. Poole.

Now, if Ms. Lubow wouldn't mind calling for a cab to take me back to the airport, I can just wait outside—"

"Young man, sit down."

Somehow he'd managed not to sputter the words. I started briefly, then blinked at him. "Is something the matter?"

"Is there some reason you have for deliberately trying to offend me? Or are you just being perverse?"

"I'm not trying to offend you. I just don't want to be your bodyguard. I realize I'm passing up a chance to go to a swell dinner and meet some people I've heard about for a long time, but that doesn't matter to me. I'm not a private eye anymore, Mr. Poole. It isn't that I don't want to bodyguard you. I don't want to bodyguard anybody."

I looked to Carla again. "If you'll call me a cab, I'd appreciate it—"

Poole interrupted me. "Mr. Donne, I'll pay triple your usual rate."

I turned back to him. "I beg your pardon?"

"I said I'll pay triple your usual rate."

"I don't have a usual rate," I said.

"Then I'll pay triple whatever your usual rate used to be."

"It used to be two hundred and fifty dollars a day," I said. "But that was a couple of years ago."

"Say three hundred a day, then. Times three."

"Nine hundred dollars a day?" I asked.

He nodded.

"I really don't think NAMES'll go for that," I said.

"I'll make up the difference from my own pocket. But you need to know, you'll be expected to watch after Miss Lubow here as well as myself. She goes wherever I go."

I considered. Nine hundred dollars a day, times the five days Peter Taylor had told me Poole was to be in Santa Ynez. Plus a free pass to the NAMES banquet. Plus spending a little more time in the company of Ms. Lubow, who at the very least was quite easy on the eyes.

I asked myself, How tough a job could it be?

I smiled at the fat man. "Mr. Poole," I said, "you've just hired yourself a bodyguard."

It was coming up on eleven-thirty by the time everything concerning the runaway Econoline had been squared away. A tow truck had been summoned to haul off the van, the cops had begun canvassing Jones Street to get the names of anyone whose parked cars may have been damaged in the ruckus, and a second cab had been dispatched to deliver my employer, his assistant, and me to the Amtrak station in Emeryville, next to Oakland.

That there wasn't an Amtrak station in San Francisco itself was one more example of what a pain in the backside this whole trip was becoming, from the moment Peter Taylor and I began making plans about how to get Poole to Santa Ynez. I'd proposed flying up to the city (as I'd done on my first visit in June), retrieving Poole and Carla in a cab, turning around, and flying back. Except Poole refused to travel in what he testily called a "puddle jumper," meaning any plane smaller than an L-1011. He hated to fly anyway—an unusual sort of phobia for somebody who did as much across- and out-of-the-country traveling as I assumed he did. Small planes only exacerbated his discomfort.

Since neither Poole nor Carla owned a car—one of the more civilized things about San Francisco being that you don't really have to in order to get around—Poole's counteroffer was for me to acquire a large enough automobile to accommodate his bulk, then drive up to the city, pick up him and his assistant, and haul us back to Santa Ynez. This time *I* balked, for two reasons. First, I was a bodyguard, not a chauffeur. Second, the thought of Poole providing me with backseat-driver advice for the duration of a six-hour ride made my stomach churn.

Peter was the one to come up with a compromise—namely, taking the train. Except there wasn't a direct Amtrak route from Santa Ynez—or Santa Barbara either, for that matter—to and from San Francisco. Somewhere along the way you have to make a bus connection—only Poole was even more adamant about not riding a bus than he was about getting on a too-tiny plane. The closest train station to Santa Ynez was Bakersfield, nearly a hundred miles away.

"How 'bout this?" Peter suggested. "You drive to Bakersfield, leave your car, and take the train to San Francisco. You pick up Poole and his assistant, come back to Bakersfield on the train, and then drive them here. It's what—an hour-and-a-half drive?"

"More like two hours," I said. Not happily.

"Still, that's better than five or six hours in the car with him. Isn't it?"

I sighed.

Having accepted the job, I had no other choice but to give in. And in fact the first leg of the trip wasn't bad at all. On Tuesday morning, I'd borrowed my uncle's Cadillac and taken a leisurely drive to Bakersfield. I caught a northbound train just after noon, and by seven o'clock that evening I was strolling into the lobby of the Hotel Nikko, where my reserved room was waiting. I phoned Carla Lubow to inform her I'd arrived, then went to the hotel restaurant to enjoy a pleasant dinner of tempura with sashimi rice, miso soup, and Japanese pickles—along with a couple of little porcelain bottles of warm sake. After dinner I took a stroll around Union Square. Returning to my room, I slipped off my shoes, plopped down on the bed, and treated myself to Hollywood's most recent mind-numbing, crash-and-burn, gazillion-dollar-budget Bruce Willis extravaganza on pay-per-view. A nice, relaxing train ride, a $200-per-night room, a $60 dinner for one? What the hell, it wasn't my money.

"WE'RE GOING TO be late," Poole uttered sourly.

He and Carla were in the backseat of the cab I'd called to replace our first one. I was riding shotgun up front, sitting beside the driver. We were tooling east, crossing the Bay Bridge. It was a beautiful, cloudless day, so sunny that the water below us sparkled.

I looked over my shoulder at Poole. I knew what he was complaining about. Ted and Peter Taylor had scheduled a dinner and reception in Poole's honor for that evening, during which he would be presented his bottle of '47 Yquem. The dinner was to commence at 8:00. By the time our 1:30 train pulled into Bakersfield, it would be 7:30. Since it would take us close to two hours to drive to Santa Ynez from there, we were indeed going to be late.

"We can still catch a plane," I offered. "We're as close to the Oakland airport as we are to the Amtrak station."

He snorted, and I turned away from him, bringing my eyes forward again.

I heard Carla say to Poole, "I phoned Peter Taylor before we left and told him what happened. He said it wouldn't be any problem moving the dinner back an hour."

Poole grunted. "We'll still be late."

"Not 'late,' " I said. "Just fashionably tardy."

Poole grunted again. "Your humor leaves a great deal to be desired, Mr. Donne. Heaven forbid that Miss Lubow and I are to be subjected to it mercilessly for the next five days."

I didn't say anything. I noticed that the cabdriver had turned around to look at me. He gave a slight nod in Poole's direction and rolled his eyes.

Tell me about it, I mouthed back to him.

We got to the Amtrak station thirty minutes before our train was to depart. I helped the cabbie unload Poole's and Carla's bags from the trunk and turned them over to a porter. Carla took care of the cab fare—I assumed it was either Poole's money she used or she had some way of expensing the fare to him. Then she gave both the driver and the porter a generous tip, which raised my esteem for her that much more. It was too bad, I was telling myself, that I already had a girlfriend back home.

The train left on time, and by 1:45 we were in a first-class compartment, rattling our way eastward. I knew from having ridden the opposite route yesterday that we would go all the way to Stockton before swinging south through the San Joaquin Valley and being dumped off in Bakersfield.

We sat in a cluster of four seats facing each other. Carla and I were side by side, she at the window. Poole sat across from us, his bulk taking up one whole seat and half of the other seat next to him. None of us had spoken since we'd sat down. I was considering a trip to the club car to get something cold to drink, when Poole asked, without preamble, "Do you know the Taylors well?"

"Are you talking to me?" I asked.

He scowled. "Since neither Miss Lubow nor I have ever met them, then yes, I'm talking to you."

I let pass the snide tone of his remark. "Fairly well. I've known Peter since we were kids."

"Tell me about them."

I shrugged, recalling what history I knew about Peter and his family. "Is it all right if I skip most of the part before they came to Santa Ynez, since I wasn't really acquainted with them then?"

"Whatever you wish."

I nodded. "From what I remember, Ted first bought the property back in the early sixties, with some money he'd inherited from some rich relative back east. At the time he was a professor of history at UCSB." I paused. "To talk to him you'd never guess he was a Ph.D. He's probably the most down-to-earth egghead I've ever met."

Poole impatiently waved a chubby hand: Whatever.

I continued. "Anyway, he and his wife, Joyce, bought a big parcel of land—more than 1,900 acres altogether—near the junction of Highways 154 and 246. At the time they were living in Goleta, near the university. They knew the land was available because they used to come up to the valley for vacations. To Lake Cachuma."

"What about their winery?" asked Poole. "I had no idea they'd been running it for so long. More than thirty years."

I shook my head. "Ted didn't start that up right away. Whenever he and Joyce and Peter had a free moment in those days, they'd come up to work the property, but they didn't make a permanent move until about twenty or so years ago, after he retired from teaching. That's when they established the winery." Another pause. "You know where the name comes from, don't you? Rancho Calzada?"

"I'm afraid not."

"It's short for El Rancho de las Calzadas. 'Ranch of the Highways.' Because of the junction right at the corner of their property." I smiled. "It sounds a lot more romantic in Spanish than it does in English."

That earned me another skip-on-down gesture from Poole.

"There's not a whole lot more to tell," I said. "They own nearly two thousand acres of some of the choicest real estate in southern California. On about a tenth of it they grow grapes. They manufacture a bunch of different wines—all of them at least palatable, some of them damn good. Everything from pinot noir to sauvignon blanc, some from their own fruit, some from fruit they buy from other growers. They've got a ranch house, a visitors' center attached to the winery, a good-size picnic grounds, and a first-class dining facility. I can assure you they are wonderful hosts—they'll feed you, bed you, and make you as comfortable as they possibly can. They also happen to be some of the nicest people I know."

I paused once again. Poole had folded his hands atop his massive belly and closed his eyes and was blowing his cheeks in and out in the same manner he'd done the first day I met him. At first I thought I'd put him to sleep, until he muttered, keeping his eyes closed, "Please go on. I'm listening."

"That's all there is," I said.

He nodded—dipping his chin one time.

"Now it's your turn," I said.

His eyes opened, and he regarded me with curiosity. "I beg your pardon?"

"It's your turn," I repeated. "To answer something for me."

His eyes narrowed. I noticed that Carla was also looking at me warily.

I said, "How do you know somebody's trying to kill you?"

Before Poole could reply, Carla cut in. "Is it really necessary for you to have an answer to that?"

I was about to reply when I happened to catch a glimpse of Poole's reaction to her question. His own wary expression had become a look of puzzled surprise. Whether he was surprised by the question or by the fact that she'd spoken at all, given that the conversation about the Taylors so far had been entirely between him and me, I didn't know.

I said to Carla, "I think it is, don't you? Given that Mr. Poole is paying me an awful lot of money just to keep an eye on him?"

She seemed to be losing her temper. "If Mr. Poole says someone's trying to kill him, then I think you should just take his word for it."

I was starting to feel a little testy myself. "It's not that I don't believe him. But it might be helpful if I had some idea of a direction where that might be coming from, so I know which way to look."

Poole barked, "Enough." He'd issued the command to both of us. Carla and I turned to him. "Mr. Donne's correct," he continued. "He has every right to know what's happened. Especially if it can give him an idea of what he might possibly expect."

She sputtered, "But Mr. Poole—"

He held up a paw to silence her. She sat back against her seat, shot me a brief if-looks-could-kill, then turned away to stare angrily out the window at the passing scenery.

Poole studied me briefly, making sure he had my full attention once again. "I told you before, there were two attempts. The first attempt was in May. We—that is to say, Miss Lubow and I—had been invited up to Calistoga to visit Schramsberg. They asked me if I would come and taste some of their new wines." He paused. "Are you familiar with Schramsberg?"

"I've had some of their stuff," I said. "It's not bad. But I prefer my sparkling wine to actually come from France. Then again, who doesn't?"

"Indeed," he said. "I presume you know your way around Napa Valley?"

"I've been there."

"So you've driven Highway 29? Up through the wine country?"

"Many times." I knew what he was referring to: the state highway that serves as the main drag through Napa, the area that pops into most people's minds when they think of California wines. SR 29 lies along the valley floor, from the town of Vallejo at the southern end, winding northwest for some thirty miles to the base of Storybook Mountain. That most people think of Napa as the only place in the state where wine comes from is understandable, since there are about 150 wineries along the stretch, surrounded by some 30,000 acres of vineyards.

Poole said, "Then you're aware that the trip can be treacherous at times?"

I nodded. "Especially when you find yourself on the road with a bunch of tourists who've done nothing but tour wineries and swill wine all day long."

"Exactly." He paused, remembering. "It was a Saturday. We'd hired a car for the day to take us to and from San Francisco. By the time we were heading back to the city, it was dark. We were a few miles north of the junction of I-80, and we'd noticed few other travelers on the road, besides ourselves." He frowned. "Until someone came up from behind, very fast, weaving back and forth. They tailgated us for a while, then ran us off the highway into a ditch."

I heard Carla issue a rather ladylike snort of disbelief. Poole glared at her. I turned to see that she was still facing the window.

I turned back to Poole. "You think whoever did it was trying to run you off the road deliberately?"

"Of course," he said.

"Ms. Lubow seems to disagree."

He waved a hand of dismissal, and she snorted again. I asked her, "How come you don't think it was deliberate?"

"It was just some drunken fool in too big a hurry, that's all," she said.

"But it did happen?"

She shrugged. "It happened."

I said to Poole, "Did you get a good look at the vehicle? Or happen to notice its license plate number?"

"Unfortunately, no."

"Then I'm afraid I'd have to agree with Ms. Lubow's assessment of the situation. That's the simplest explanation for what happened. If there's one thing I learned from working in law enforcement, it's that nine times out of ten, the simplest explanation is the right one."

Poole nodded. "I thought so myself, until the second attempt."

"The second attempt on your life?"

He nodded. "Someone tried to shoot me."

I narrowed my eyes. "Shoot you?"

"It was on a Friday, two weeks after the incident in Napa. We were on our way to lunch at the Garden Court at the Sheraton Palace downtown. I was just getting out of the taxi when I heard a gunshot, and the window of the door I was opening was shattered."

"You're sure it was a gunshot?"

He looked insulted. "I know what one sounds like, Mr. Donne. Besides, the police found the bullet on the floor of the cab. From a .38-caliber handgun, they said."

"The police filed a report?"

Poole made a face. "For all the good it did. They had no idea where the shot may have come from. A passing car, most likely."

"You never saw anything?"

He shook his head.

I turned to Carla. "Can I assume, when Mr. Poole says 'we' were going to lunch, he's referring to you, too?"

She looked at me but said nothing.

"Were you there or weren't you?" I asked.

"I was there."

"And?"

"It happened just like Mr. Poole said. I heard the shot, and I saw the window break, but that was all."

"You didn't see anybody in a car with a gun, anything like that?"

"No."

I turned to Poole again. "What did the police say?"

Another wave of dismissal. "Bah. A random act of urban violence. The fools."

"Your basic drive-by shooting?"

"According to them."

"But you don't agree?"

"Someone's trying to kill me," he said flatly. "That's why I've hired you to protect me."

So there. He'd made up his mind he was a target for assassination, and it would be useless to try to convince him otherwise.

"Just for the record," I said, "you don't want me to put any effort into finding out who it is that might dislike you enough to want to see you dead, do you? You just want me to help keep you and Ms. Lubow alive through Sunday?"

"That's all I want," he said.

"Good," I said. " 'Cause that's all you're going to get."

arla had brought along a picnic basket containing our lunch, prepared by Poole's personal chef, a man named Timothy Kempel, whom I'd met that morning. He'd made us chicken curry sandwiches on rosemary bread, with some smoked Gouda and fresh fruit on the side. He'd even included a couple of bottles of J. B. Adam's '92 pinot blanc to wash everything down.

It was a very nice lunch, even if we did have to eat it from our laps. To my delight, Kempel had remembered to pack some white-wine glasses along with the plastic plates and dinnerware. While we were eating, I amused myself by imagining Poole reduced to choking down some cellophane-wrapped, processed-ham-and-processed-cheese-on-white-bread abomination, a bag of Fritos, and a can of Coke—which is what our meal would have been if we'd been forced to rely on what Amtrak provided.

After the meal Poole and Carla had some correspondence to attend to, via Carla's laptop PC. When she coolly mentioned that their business was personal, I moved to an open seat across the aisle from them, out of earshot.

I'd brought along a paperback novel by Michael Connelly,

whose hero was an obsessive LAPD detective named Harry Bosch. The story was interesting enough, about Bosch's attempt to unravel a thirty-year-old murder—his mother's—but for some reason I kept reading the same page over and over.

Then I figured out why. In the back of my mind I was trying to dope out if I believed somebody was really trying to kill Augustus Poole.

The rational part of me said no. What I'd told Poole about the simplest explanation nearly always being the right one held fast. If you treated the two incidents separately—the hit-and-run encounter on Highway 29 and the potshot in downtown San Francisco—each had a perfectly simple explanation.

But if you put them together, I asked myself, did that make for too much of a coincidence?

I shook my head, deciding that Poole's paranoia must be catching. All I had to do was baby-sit him till Sunday, and Raymond Donne's one-and-only favorite son would be a cool forty-five hundred bucks richer. If Poole went anywhere by car in the next few days, I'd be the one behind the wheel. And if there'd ever been a drive-by shooting in the Santa Ynez Valley, it had escaped the notice of everybody I knew who'd ever lived there. End of discussion.

THERE'S NO SUCH thing as a direct route from Bakersfield to the Santa Ynez Valley. From the train station you get on I-5 and head south to pick up Highway 166 going west, and then you drive a long stretch of two-lane blacktop along the northern base of the Sierra Madre Mountains. Eventually you reach Highway 101, just outside the city of Santa Maria. You go south on 101, then angle southeast on Highway 154. At the junction of the 101 and the 154 is San Tomas, where my dad and I live. The town of

Santa Ynez—at the eastern edge of which sits Rancho Calzada—
is a bit farther down the road.

All told, the trip is around 120 miles. If I'd been by myself
in my Jeep Cherokee, I could have cut a little time and distance
by employing a pretty hairy shortcut that crosses over the Sierra Madres to the valley. As I didn't think Poole's disposition—
nor my uncle's Cadillac—could tolerate it, I took the careful
route.

Nevertheless, we made decent time, arriving at Rancho
Calzada an hour or so after nightfall, around 9:45 P.M. The party
was in full swing. The Taylors had hired a valet parking service
all the way from Santa Barbara—which was good, because as I
guided the Seville up Rancho Calzada's driveway I couldn't see
a parking spot anywhere.

Most of the NAMES attendees were staying at various hotels
and motels and B&Bs around the valley, since the Taylors' com-
pound included only four guest bungalows for overnight visitors.
Peter had apprised me of the room assignments: one bungalow
was for Poole, one for Carla, one for NAMES' president Michael
Gottberg, and one for Niccolo Paoletti, the man who'd be super-
vising the preparation of every meal served here over the next
couple of days, including the banquet on Saturday night.

I asked Poole if he and Carla wanted to see their rooms and
unpack before they headed over to join the festivities. "That can
wait," he responded vehemently. I knew why he was being so
insistent. As I helped him out of the car, I was recalling that for
the last twenty miles I'd been hearing the rumble of his stomach
all the way up in the driver's seat.

I left the Cadillac with an attendant, then led Poole and Carla
up a flagstone walkway to the banquet room. They probably
could have found it on their own by following the wallah of noisy,
genial conversation. I held open a door, admitting them into what

looked to be nothing more than a large cocktail party—sixty or so people, all on their feet, gathered in clumps of varying number. They were enjoying drinks and hors d'oeuvres, served by a squadron of white-jacketed waitpersons. I felt a wash of satisfaction that we'd made it before dinner was served. One less thing for Mr. Poole to bitch about.

As I was closing the door behind us, I heard Peter Taylor's voice calling: "Jack! You're here!"

Poole, Carla, and I turned to Peter, who'd broken away from a couple of people I didn't know. I could tell from my friend's grin as he approached us that my pleasure at having arrived in time for dinner had nothing on his relief at my getting Poole there at all.

I provided introductions, intercepting the hand Peter extended to Poole as I repeated Carla's explanation about how her boss disliked being touched. By now the room had quieted, everyone becoming aware that the guest of honor was present.

Peter guided Poole away from Carla and me to introduce him around, while I signaled a waiter to get a glass of wine for Carla and me and something for us to nibble on. I asked the waiter how long it was going to be till the sit-down food would be served, and he assured me that it was on its way. Poole's stomach hadn't been the only one growling.

THE WAY IT worked, whoever hosted the annual NAMES affair was responsible for supplying all of the group's meals. If the host happened to be a chef himself (or herself, though the organization had only about a dozen female members), it was no problem. If you were the owner of a restaurant, you had your people do the cooking. If, like the Taylors, you weren't in the food preparation business, you had to bring somebody in.

I'd met Niccolo Paoletti on a couple of occasions, but he was barely a casual acquaintance. When Peter informed me he'd been chosen by the Taylors to be responsible for the NAMES meals at Rancho Calzada, I had no trouble approving the choice. Paoletti was as esteemed as any chef on the West Coast, operating out of a ritzy establishment called the Courtyard Café in Montecito. Roger Platt, the fellow who owned the Courtyard, had won a whole pile of awards over the years, and he also enjoyed a four-star rating in the most recent Michelin guide, among other publications, due to Nicky Paoletti's talents.

If Paoletti's menu for tonight's "simple" late supper was any clue, then Saturday's banquet was going to be a barn burner. He'd wisely kept the courses light—cream of lima bean soup with bits of bacon, a tomato salad with hard-boiled eggs, broiled chicken wings for the main course, and poached pears with chocolate sauce for dessert. As a rule I don't like to eat too late in the evening, because I hate to go to bed feeling like I'm going to pop. That wasn't a problem this evening at all. The food wasn't overly filling, merely terrific.

Ten of the circular tables in the room had been set for six diners each. I was at a table toward the back. Seated to my left was Carla Lubow. The only other person I knew at my table was Terry Elliott, my uncle's golfing buddy, who sat to my right. One seat at our table was empty. The other two people with us—a man and a woman, the former from New York City, the latter from Miami—had been introduced to me as NAMES members, though I quickly forgot their names. Rude of me, I suppose, but there you are.

I spent most of the meal attempting to make small talk with Carla, who still seemed miffed at me for the little verbal altercation we'd had during our train ride. I tried questioning her about what life with Poole was like—how long she'd been associated with him, what exactly her duties entailed, how difficult it must be to travel with him overseas if he was as much a pain on a long trip as he'd been on the short one we'd just had.

Her answers couldn't have been more perfunctory. She'd been Poole's personal assistant for four years. In addition to the usual secretarial duties, her job included taking charge of Poole's schedule and handling his correspondence. She supervised the layout and publication of his newsletter. She also assured me that, in spite of evidence to the contrary, Poole actually enjoyed traveling overseas—most recently to Japan, where they'd made three trips over the past eighteen months. According to Carla, a number of well-heeled Japanese wine collectors regarded Augustus Poole as a font of enological expertise, and they paid him large fees to come over and advise them how to spend more of their money than what they'd already spent on him.

"Well, fancy that," I said.

I probably should have kept the sarcasm out of my voice. Carla sneered, then turned her back to me. She and the woman next to her commenced an entirely new conversation that I wasn't meant to have any part in.

I was about to start in on my dessert when I heard the *tink-tink-tink* of someone tapping on a water glass. Along with everyone else, I turned toward the front of the room. A long, rectangular table had been set up on a raised dais. The table was for the big kids: Joyce, Peter, and Ted Taylor; Michael Gottberg; Augustus Poole. Behind the dais to one side was the doorway to the kitchen. I could see Nicky Paoletti there, watching everyone enjoy the meal he'd prepared.

The man who'd tapped on a glass was Gottberg. I'd never laid eyes on him before, knowing him only by reputation as the sommelier of a place called Scallops up in Seattle, Washington.

Like everybody else in NAMES, though, Gottberg was highly thought of in the food and wine business.

He was a nondescript-looking guy—an inch, give or take, above average height, brown hair, neatly trimmed beard. "Can I please have everyone's attention?" he called out to the room. There followed a brief rustle of shifting bodies and squeak of chairs being moved that quieted quickly enough.

"First of all," he continued, "I'd like to thank the Taylors for their tremendous hospitality. It's hard for me to imagine a more genial setting for this year's banquet. Thank you, Ted and Joyce and Peter."

Gottberg led everyone in applauding the Taylors, and I was happy to join in. Ted rose halfway from his chair and waved to the assembled group.

When the applause subsided, Gottberg turned to indicate the man behind him in the kitchen doorway. "And of course, thanks to Niccolo Paoletti for providing such a wonderful meal tonight. I for one am looking forward to the banquet on Saturday, if tonight's meal was only a sample of what's to come."

More applause, and even a few whistles of appreciation. Paoletti took a bow.

"And last but not least," said Gottberg, "our guest speaker, Mr. Augustus Poole."

I registered that the assembly's expression of appreciation for Poole was somewhat less enthusiastic than it had been for the Taylors or Nicky Paoletti. Poole acknowledged it with the merest dip of his head. As the token applause died away, Gottberg was saying, "Now. To make a very special presentation to Mr. Poole, I'd like to turn over the proceedings to our host, Ted Taylor."

Another brief round of applause. As Ted stood up, Terry Elliott leaned over to me and whispered, "There goes my wine."

I nodded, smiling, and whispered back, "That was awfully generous of you."

He shrugged. "The society paid me for it. They actually saved a little money. It cost 'em less for the wine than they'd have spent on the speaker's fee. Besides, I still have one bottle left."

"So I heard."

I'd been forewarned by Peter that his father had a prepared speech he was going to give tonight before handing over the bottle of '47 Yquem. According to Peter, the speech was going to be short. That Ted's topic was Augustus Poole, though, didn't fill me with an edge-of-my-seat desire to hang on his every word.

As Ted began to drone about Poole's lofty position in the epicurean community, I leaned over to Terry Elliott. I pointed with my chin to indicate that we should move away a little, so as not to bother our tablemates. Terry and I scooted our chairs a few feet from everyone else, then leaned in close to hear one another.

Terry, who is about the same age as my uncle, looked at me with a questioning expression. I whispered, "How come Poole didn't just take the money? He could have bought his own bottle of '47 Yquem and still have a few bucks left over."

"Assuming he could find a bottle for sale," Terry whispered back. "It's not like there's a lot available to the general public." He paused. "I'd be surprised if there's more than a few dozen bottles of '47 Yquem left in the world. I can't speak for anyone else, but I know if Poole had come to me and tried to buy one of mine, I'd've turned him down cold. Just on principle."

My turn to look puzzled.

"I'd never have sold a bottle to Augustus Poole directly," Terry explained. "Not for any amount of money. But the way I see it, I'm just doing a favor for NAMES. I may not like Poole, but I like the people in the organization." He grinned. "Most of 'em, anyway."

The other people in the room started to applaud again. Terry and I politely joined in. I noticed that Poole was lifting his considerable bulk from his seat, getting up to cross to where Ted Taylor was cradling the sauternes in his hands.

Still clapping, Terry leaned in to me. "I may not like the man, but I got to admit he has good taste in wine. He made a helluva choice."

"The '47's really that great?"

The applause died away as Poole accepted his tribute from Ted. Terry and I stopped clapping as well. "You've never tasted it?" Terry whispered.

"Not the '47," I said. "I've had some of the more recent big ones—'75 and '76, maybe a couple others. I'm actually not that hot on dessert wines."

"Too bad," said Terry. " 'Forty-seven Yquem's one of the all-time champs, believe me. Real nectar of the gods. I'm not exaggerating." He smiled. "Maybe I should have you and your uncle and your dad over some time, and we'll open my last bottle."

I smiled back. "Any time you say—"

I was interrupted by a sudden commotion at the front of the room. Several of the diners were getting up out of their chairs, and Terry and I did likewise, our attention drawn toward the dais. As soon as I saw who was involved, I muttered to myself, "Good God, what now?"

Then I was hurrying toward the front table, Carla Lubow alongside me. A noisy fracas had erupted between Poole and Nicky Paoletti. The two men were being bodily separated— Poole held back by Ted and Peter Taylor, Paoletti by Michael Gottberg.

As Carla and I neared, Poole's and Paoletti's angry shouts

resolved themselves into more or less sensible—if profane—speech. Paoletti was reproaching Poole for being ungracious, greedy, and selfish. Poole was tossing it right back, accusing the chef of being a no-talent hack who didn't belong in the kitchen of a hash house, much less a four-star dining establishment.

The decibel level was escalating, and several of the other diners were starting to form a crowd. I considered my options, one of which was to turn around and go home. Instead I put two fingers in my mouth and whistled as loudly and shrilly as I could.

The shouting immediately ceased. Everybody in the room had their eyes on me. I waited a beat for the quiet to settle, then asked politely, "What in the hell is going on here?"

Both Poole and Paoletti started in on me simultaneously. I whistled again for silence. I turned to Paoletti. "Nicky? You first."

Paoletti was a slender, olive-skinned man and not at all imposing in any physical way. But he was also native-born Italian, and he possessed a stereotypical Italian temper. And an accent to boot.

He was quivering with rage, pointing an accusatory finger at Poole. "This—this glutton! All I did was suggest it would be polite of him to open his precious wine and share it with some of us who provided him this wonderful meal! It was a perfectly reasonable request! And he—!"

I held up a hand to quiet him, then turned to my employer. "Mr. Poole?"

He took a moment to straighten his clothes and summon up his dignity. Then he blinked and lifted his shoulders in a kind of indifferent shrug. "What this—person says is substantially correct. He asked me if he could have a sample of my sauternes, and I told him no."

Paoletti went off like a Roman candle once again, and I had to whistle a third time.

As soon as the silence resettled, I looked to Poole. "It's getting late," I told him. "I think it's time for you to go to your room."

He seemed about to sputter something more, but decided better of it. He nodded. "After you, Mr. Donne." He motioned to Carla Lubow, who'd been standing next to me the entire time. "Shall we, my dear?"

The crowd parted to let us exit. As we approached the door, I noticed that the corners of Poole's mouth were turned up in an impish smile. As soon as we got outside, he said to me in a voice touched with amusement, "Been rather an exciting day, wouldn't you say, Mr. Donne?"

"I don't know if 'exciting' is quite the word I'd use," I said grumpily, not bothering to tell him how glad I was that the damned day at last seemed to be over. Thank God.

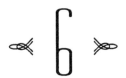

Rancho Calzada's four guest bungalows were arranged in a three-quarter circle at the end of a footpath a few hundred yards from the winery's main building, where the dining room, kitchen, tasting room, and office space were housed. Peter helped me lug Poole's and Carla's bags from the car. It didn't take long to get them settled in their digs, but as I was climbing into my uncle's Caddy to head for home, I noticed the digital clock on the dashboard. It was 1:15 A.M. Fatigue washed over me like a wave at the realization of what a long, long day it had been. A headache began to pulse over my right eyebrow. Swell. Only four more days to go.

Were I in my Cherokee, I probably could have made it home on autopilot. As it was I needed to crank on the Caddy's CD player at high volume to keep myself alert. Knowing I was going to have my uncle's car for the next several days and not completely trusting Gerry's taste, I'd stocked a bunch of my own music. One of the items I'd brought along was a two-disc set of the Allman Brothers Band live at the Fillmore East, circa 1971, which I'd picked up a month or so ago and had been listening to lately with religious fervor. I speak from personal experience when I say "Whipping Post" played very loud goes a long way toward keeping you awake if you're driving drowsy.

As I expected, the house was dark when I got home. People who operate agrarian businesses—not just vintners, but ranchers and farmers and such—are, as a rule, early-to-bed-early-to-rise sorts. My father is no exception, and generally neither am I— another reason why I felt so exhausted. When I was with BATF, working undercover, I used to be a real night owl. These days if I went to bed later than 11:00 P.M. or slept in past seven in the morning, I'd be nonfunctional.

I entered the house and padded to the kitchen as quietly as I could. Though I'd had plenty to drink over the past twelve hours—wine with lunch on the train, a cocktail, and then a few more glasses of wine with dinner—I was feeling the need for a nightcap. I reasoned that anyone who spent as much time in Augustus Poole's company as I did today was entitled to drink. Heavily.

I switched on the kitchen light, then crossed to the cabinet where Dad and I keep a supply of aperitifs and after-dinner cordials. I found what I was looking for, a bottle of Domecq amontillado we'd opened the other night. After pulling down a sherry glass from another cabinet, I poured myself a healthy slug, returned the bottle to its place, then went over to the kitchen table to sit and sip.

On the table was a note for me from Dad. Margaret McKenney, a.k.a. Maggie, had telephoned around 8:00 P.M, wanting to know if I'd made it back okay and if I had Augustus Poole in tow. Maggie is Donne Vineyards' accountant. She also happens to be my girlfriend, the one on whose account I knew better than to make any actual play for Carla Lubow.

Maggie is a genuine Irish colleen—a red-haired, green-eyed,

freckle-skinned beauty a few years younger than I—with a feisty Irish temper. Ever since we started seeing one another over a year ago, I hadn't felt the urge to go hounding after any other women, so I don't really have any hard evidence as to how deep or wide a jealous streak she might possess. But I'd been on the receiving end of her wrath on any number of occasions, often enough that it would be foolish to tempt fate. Especially since I didn't really have a desire to be involved with anybody else anyway.

Since Dad's note didn't imply that I needed to respond the moment I got home, it was an easy decision to wait till morning to return Maggie's call. I finished my nightcap, then went over to the sink to rinse my glass and put it on the drying rack. After making sure the kitchen was as tidy as it had been when I came in, I switched off the light and headed down the hallway to my bedroom. I closed the bedroom door behind me before turning on the light, then stripped out of my clothes and went to my bathroom for a quick shower. Maybe I could wash away the tension from my neck and shoulders, thereby enabling myself to sleep like the proverbial rock.

No such luck. Falling asleep isn't usually a problem for me, but as I lay in my bed in the darkness, the day's events kept replaying. The runaway van, the long train ride, the drive from Bakersfield, the dinner culminating the scuffle between Poole and Nicky Paoletti—over and over the scenes unreeled.

I hoped it wasn't an indication I'd have insomnia for the entire time Poole was in Santa Ynez. All of a sudden, $4,500 didn't seem worth it. Not anymore.

I HAVE NO idea when I finally fell asleep, but it was just after sunrise when I woke up, jarred to consciousness by the harsh ringing of the phone on the night table next to my bed. I judged the time by the gray early-morning light filtering into my bedroom, and a glance at my bedside clock to confirm my judgment made me groan. It was 5:35 A.M.

I picked up the phone and grunted as polite a greeting as I could manage, given the circumstances.

"Mr. Donne?"

It was a female voice I couldn't place, until she said, "It's Carla Lubow."

It wasn't difficult to register the urgency in her voice. I was immediately wide awake. "What's the matter?"

"You need to get over here right away."

"Where are you?"

"Rancho Calzada." A pause. "Something terrible's happened. Someone—somebody's been—"

"Is something wrong with Poole?"

"No, no, not Mr. Poole. It's that other man, the chef. Niccolo Paoletti. Something's happened to him."

"Nicky?"

She took a deep breath. "I think someone may have poisoned him."

"Poisoned him—?"

"Could you please just get over here as soon as you can? The police are already on their way."

"The police?"

"Mr. Poole had me call them first, before I called you. Right after he found the body."

My head was spinning. "Wait a minute, wait a minute. *Poole* found the body?"

"Please, Mr. Donne, can you just get over here?"

What else could I do? "I'll be there in thirty minutes," I said.

. . .

AS I WAS getting dressed, I heard a knock on my bedroom door. "Come on in," I called.

Dad pushed open the door and stood on the threshold, dressed in pajamas and bathrobe, supporting himself on his cane. He had a grumpy scowl on his face, no doubt from having been awakened by the phone. "Who in God's name is calling you at five-thirty in the morning?"

"Carla Lubow, Augustus Poole's assistant."

"What's she want?"

"Apparently somebody over at Rancho Calzada just got poisoned."

His scowl evaporated and his mouth dropped open. "You're kidding."

"I wish I was," I said, pulling on my shoes.

As I came out of the house, I noticed that the sun was all the way up, hanging over the eastern horizon like an angry orange eye. There wasn't a cloud in the sky, and I could tell by the feel of the air on my skin that today was going to be a scorcher. I hoped it wasn't an omen, like my insomnia, that things weren't going to go well.

It was a foolish hope, since I already knew that Nicky Paoletti was dead, maybe poisoned, and that my client was somehow involved. I started the Cadillac and turned the air conditioner on full, telling myself not to make any further judgments till I'd had a chance to file away a few more facts.

Highway 154 was all but deserted in both directions, most people having the good sense to still be in bed at this hour. As I rolled onto the Rancho Calzada property, I saw a pair of Santa Barbara County Sheriff's patrol cars parked at the top of the drive, one alongside the other. I couldn't see any human beings moving about, but I assumed they wouldn't be hard to find, since they were probably all gathered at the scene of the disaster.

I parked away from the prowl cars, then went along the footpath toward the guest bungalows. The front door of one of the four bungalows was open. A uniformed deputy sheriff was outside the door, unreeling a roll of crime scene tape. He looked up at the sound of my footsteps, and his eyes narrowed suspiciously—a look so common to law enforcement types that many people must think it's the first thing they teach you in cop school. Before I could introduce myself and explain what I was doing there, I heard Poole bellowing, "Mr. Donne!"

I stopped and turned around. Poole was standing on the threshold of his own bungalow across the way. He was dressed in sleepwear—a goldenrod-colored dressing gown made of silk over a pair of bright yellow pajamas of the same material. His feet were shod in black calfskin slippers that covered his toes but left his heels bare. He was glaring at me, arms folded defiantly across his massive torso.

I turned to the deputy. "I'll be right back," I said, giving him a little wave.

He grunted and resumed unrolling his tape. "Take your time. It ain't like anybody's going anywhere."

"Including me," I said.

He grunted something else, but by then I was on my way to Poole's bungalow. Poole had already disappeared inside, leaving the door open. I assumed that was an invitation, so I crossed the short path to his doorstep and went on in.

Each of the guest bungalows at Rancho Calzada was exactly the same: a two-room suite—living room and bedroom—with a decent-size bathroom attached to the latter. The rooms were functional and comfortable and clean, but little more than that. It wasn't the Ritz Carlton, but neither was it a Motel Six.

I entered the living room and closed the door. Poole had taken a seat on the biggest piece of furniture in the room, a long sofa that lay against the wall to the left as you came in the front door. He was gasping, as if the exertion of going all the way outside to summon me had left him out of breath. He waved me to a matching chair near the end of the sofa.

"Where's Miss Lubow?" I asked, taking my seat.

"In her bungalow, getting dressed."

"What about the Taylors? Has anybody told them that the cops are crawling all over their property?"

"They're also getting dressed. Miss Lubow's informed them that she'd notified you as well."

"You might want to do that yourself," I said. "Get dressed, I mean. Those pajamas aren't fit for public display. They make you look like an overgrown canary."

He snorted, waving a dismissive hand. "Bah! I'll dress presently. First you need to be made aware of what's happened."

I settled back and drummed my fingers on the arm of the chair, looking around the room absently. "I hear you found a body."

He scowled, more or less the reaction I'd expected. He motioned toward the cottage. "Paoletti."

"Maybe you'd better start with what happened after I went home last night."

He grunted again. "Maybe if you'd been here doing your job instead of going home, none of this would have happened."

"None of what would have happened?"

He took in about a quart of air that he let out again in a long sigh. "Do you remember when you and Mr. Taylor—the younger one—brought me here? The two of you carried my luggage for me?"

"I remember."

"Do you remember what I was carrying?"

"Your '47 Yquem," I said. "You were holding on to it for dear life."

He nodded, disregarding my little gibe. "I took it in the bedroom with me and placed it on a shelf in the closet. After you and Mr. Taylor left, I locked the front door behind you. Then I got ready for bed. I put on my pajamas and robe, and I sat up for a while in here, reading."

He paused again, studying me as if to make sure I was paying attention. "Go on," I told him.

"Around two-thirty I suddenly felt hungry. Mr. Taylor—the elder one, not the younger—told me while we were on the dais I could make myself at home as long as I was here."

"Didn't I say they were hospitable?"

"Indeed. I put on my slippers and robe and went out to find the kitchen where our meal had been prepared."

"I imagine that wasn't too difficult," I said. "Since it's right next to the dining room."

Either he'd grown accustomed to my digs or he'd made up his mind to ignore them. "I took some leftover chicken wings from the refrigerator. I also had a glass of milk." He made a gesture encompassing the living room. "I was gone for perhaps half an hour, then I came right back here."

"Is that significant?" I asked. "How long you were out of your bungalow?"

He nodded. "As I say, I was gone for about half an hour. After which I came directly back here and went straight to bed."

"Then what happened?"

Another deep breath. "I fell asleep. Only not for very long. I woke up an hour or so later with the oddest feeling that something was wrong. I don't know how I knew, but . . ."

His voice trailed off. "Knew what?" I asked.

He scowled again. "Someone had taken my sauternes."

"Come again?"

"My Yquem. Somebody'd stolen it. I got up out of bed,

switched on the light, and hurried to the closet. Sure enough, it was gone."

"Gone?"

"Gone. Missing. No longer where I'd left it." Another pause. "At first I considered whether I might have moved it somewhere else myself, but of course I hadn't. I searched the entire cottage, just to make sure it was nowhere to be found. But while I was searching, I realized what must have happened."

"That's when you decided somebody stole it?"

He nodded adamantly. "While I was out getting my snack."

He was about to continue, when I held up a hand to stifle him. "Let me guess," I said. "It only took you two seconds to figure out who that 'somebody' had to be."

"It was obvious, don't you think? Who else could possibly have done it?"

"Nicky Paoletti," I said.

"I WAS FRANTIC, I admit that," continued Poole. "Not to mention enraged."

"Not to mention."

He scowled yet again. "It annoys me that you're not taking this very seriously, Mr. Donne. We're talking about a priceless bottle of wine."

"Aren't we also talking about murder?" I said. "It seems to me that's a little more serious than losing a bottle of wine, no matter how much it might be worth."

His forehead furrowed, and his expression became about as close to chagrin as I supposed he could manage. "You're right, of course."

"Then can we cut to the chase, please?"

He nodded. "I put on my robe and slippers again and rushed

over to Paoletti's bungalow. I should have suspected something was amiss when I noticed that the lights were on inside, but I was much too angry to think straight. If anything, the fact that the lights were on indicated to me that I was correct. He was still awake, probably sipping my wine at that very moment. I went up and pounded on his door, but there was no reply. I twisted the knob, not expecting the door to be unlocked, but it was."

"The door was open?"

He nodded. "I was just as surprised then as you are now. Enough so that my anger subsided a bit. I could also feel the hairs on the back of my neck starting to tickle. And I noticed an odor— a very foul smell."

"What was it?"

He made a face. "It was—how can I say this delicately?"

"Don't bother," I said. "Just tell me."

His face creased with distaste. "Like an open sewer, only worse. As if someone had defecated somewhere close by. As if they—"

I gestured for him to stop. "I get the picture. Then what happened?"

"I opened the door."

"And?"

"And there was Paoletti. On the floor. Dead."

"You're sure of that? That he was dead?"

"I stared at him for several moments," Poole said. "He wasn't breathing. He wasn't moving at all, for that matter."

"You didn't happen to touch him, did you?"

"Heavens, no!"

"What did you do?"

"When I was finally able to gather my composure, I went over to Miss Lubow's bungalow and woke her up. I told her what had happened, and that she should go up to the Taylors' house and wake them up, then use the phone to call the police. And you."

"You're sure she was asleep?" I asked. "Carla, I mean?"

He looked puzzled. "Of course she was asleep. She—"

He paused. A look of realization crossed his face, then he gave me another scowl. "You can't possibly believe she had anything to do with this."

"I'm just gathering information," I said. "It's a policy of mine. The more I know now, the less stupid I tend to appear when somebody asks me about something later on."

He seemed to accept that. "Then, yes, I woke her out of a sound sleep. And I noticed no indication that she'd been out of her cottage since we'd said our good-nights. Satisfied?"

I didn't respond right away; something else had just occurred to me. Poole must have registered the dark expression on my face, because he asked, "What's the matter?"

"I just thought of something," I said. "When Carla phoned me, she said Paoletti had been poisoned."

"So?"

"So how did she know that?"

The question earned me another of Poole's you-must-be-an-idiot looks. "I told her, of course."

"But how did *you* know? That's really the question."

"Well, because—"

He froze, looking bewildered, until the lightbulb went on over his head. "I see. Up till now I hadn't mentioned a word about how Paoletti might have died. But the fact that I have any idea at all may be evidence that I'm the one who actually killed him. That's what you're considering, isn't it?"

"Something like that."

"I suppose I've no reason to be upset with you, since it's a perfectly reasonable assumption."

"I'm glad you think so," I said. "Now, how 'bout answering the question."

"It's a simple explanation," said Poole. "Since I found my bottle of sauternes lying—"

He was interrupted by a couple of sharp raps on the front door. He glanced at the door, then turned back to me with a questioning look.

"My guess it's either Carla, one of the Taylors, or somebody from the sheriff's department," I said. "Would you like me to find out?"

He nodded. I got up, crossed to the door, and pulled it open.

The weary-looking fellow who'd knocked was standing on the threshold. A couple of years younger, a few inches shorter, and many pounds lighter than I, he had a narrow nose, brown eyes, a high forehead and a sparse mustache the same reddish-brown color as his brush-cut hair. He wore what looked to be the same ugly polyester sport-coat-and-tie combination he'd been wearing the last time I'd bumped into him when he was on duty. He had out the leather case in which he carried his detective's shield and was lifting up his badge to show me when he finally registered who had opened the door.

He gaped at me. "Jesus Christ. Jack Donne. What the hell are you doing here?"

"How's it goin', Brad?" I said. "What's new?"

I'D HAD MY first professional encounter with Lieutenant Bradley Fitch of the Santa Barbara County Sheriff's Department's Detective Bureau while I was working for Ozzie Cole last April. Fitch and I had actually known each other before that, having attended San Tomas High School together more than two decades ago. We'd been on the high school baseball team together, although at the time we weren't close friends because I was a senior and one of the team's stars, and Fitch was a sophomore benchwarmer.

What I found out, upon our becoming reacquainted during the Cole affair, was that Brad Fitch had grown up hero-worshiping me. He kept tabs on my brief baseball career at San Diego State University as well as my hitch with the U.S. Air Force, and finally he imitated my entry into law enforcement by joining the sheriff's department shortly after graduating from junior college. At first I'd been a little embarrassed by Fitch's fawning—until I found out that underneath it all he was a pretty good cop. Brave, too—I knew, because barely three months before I'd waited outside to back him up while he insisted on going into a darkened building alone after an armed killer. For his trouble he'd caught a bullet in his right shoulder.

As I moved aside to usher Fitch into Poole's bungalow, I said, "So when did they put you back on active duty?"

"Two weeks ago," Fitch said. "Right after I finished rehabbing." He put his left hand on the shoulder where he'd taken the bullet, crooked his right elbow, and rotated his arm. He grinned. "See? Good as new. Some of it's plastic in there now instead of bone, but it's good as new."

"Congratulations."

"So what the hell are you doing here?"

"I could ask you the same thing."

"I happened to be catching on the graveyard shift, that's all. I'm the investigator on call. They beep me, I answer, boom: possible homicide, Rancho Calzada." He looked in the direction of the fat man on the sofa. "I'm here to talk to somebody named Augustus Poole who's supposed to be staying in this bungalow. I take it, sir, you're Mr. Poole?"

Poole dipped his head slightly.

Fitch turned back to me. "Your turn, Jack."

"What am I doing here?"

"Yeah."

"You're not going to believe it," I said, "but I'm working for Mr. Poole. Even though I swore to you it wouldn't happen, I'm doing it again."

"Doing what again?"

I sighed. "Being a damned private eye."

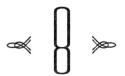

itch settled into a chair matching my own at the opposite end of the sofa. I gave him a capsule version of how I'd been hired to bodyguard Poole for the duration of his visit to Santa Ynez. I didn't go into detail as to the why; the lieutenant was more interested in querying Poole about how he'd come to discover Nicky Paoletti's dead body next door.

Fitch read Poole his Miranda rights, something that my employer found a little disconcerting until I assured him that the procedure was strictly routine. Everyone questioned in a homicide investigation is Mirandized, I told him, even when they're not suspected of the crime.

I sat patiently while Poole repeated the same story he'd just got done telling me. Fitch would occasionally press him for details that hadn't occurred to me—questions that pinned down the times when Poole was out getting his snack, when he'd awakened to find his Yquem gone, when he'd opened Paoletti's door, when he'd got Carla Lubow up, and so on. Poole never wavered from the story he'd told me, nor did anything in his manner indicate that he was being other than completely honest.

"Let's talk about this bottle of wine of yours," Fitch was saying. "What's it called again?"

"A 1947 Chateau d'Yquem," said Poole.

"And what kind of wine is that?" Fitch showed a small, apologetic smile. "You'll pardon my ignorance, Mr. Poole. Jack here is the wine maven. Me, I couldn't tell you the difference between cabernet sauvignon and Gallo Hearty Burgundy."

Poole looked mortified.

"Bear with him, Mr. Poole," I said. "He's only doing his job."

Poole gave me a brief, baleful glare, then looked to Fitch again. "Sauternes is a sweet dessert wine that comes from a small region in France. Chateau d'Yquem is generally acknowledged by experts, including myself, to be the finest producer of sauternes in the world."

Fitch asked, "And this particular vintage? Nineteen forty-seven? That's a valuable one?"

Poole nodded. "As I told Mr. Donne a short while ago, it's priceless."

"And rare, too, I assume?"

"Extremely."

Fitch asked, "So it's unlikely that the bottle in Mr. Paoletti's room is anything other than the one you say was taken from yours?"

"Whoa, whoa," I interrupted. "Slow down. You're getting ahead of me here."

"What do you mean?" asked Fitch.

I turned to Poole. "You didn't say anything to me about your wine turning up in Paoletti's room."

"I was about to," said Poole, "when Lieutenant Fitch came to the door."

"Do you mind filling me in now, if it's not too much trouble?"

He blinked, surprised by my pique. "Not at all. I told you how I opened the door and saw Paoletti lying on the floor. My sauternes was right there next to him."

"On the floor?"

"Yes."

"Opened?"

"Of course." Poole's face twisted with sorrow. "A great deal of it had spilled out."

"Did you notice anything else you haven't told me about?" I asked.

"A tumbler," said Poole. He nodded in the direction of his bungalow's bathroom. "A drinking glass. Like the one I have in there."

"Also on the floor?"

"Yes."

"Next to Paoletti's body?"

"Yes—"

Fitch cleared his throat loudly: "A-hem."

I turned to him. "Do you mind, Jack?" he said. "I'd like to be the one to handle this investigation, if it's okay with you."

"Sorry," I said.

Fitch looked to Poole. "When you opened the door and saw the body on the floor—"

"Don't forget the wine," added Poole. "And the glass."

"The wine and the glass. Did you go in?"

Poole began to answer, then hesitated. He frowned.

Fitch asked, "Did you or didn't you?"

"Well—"

I couldn't help interrupting again. "Now wait one damn minute. You just told me not half an hour ago you didn't touch anything in Paoletti's room."

"No, I didn't," insisted Poole.

"You most certainly did."

"I most certainly did not. You asked me if I'd touched the body, and I told you I didn't, which is the truth. You didn't ask me if I'd gone inside or touched anything else."

"Damn it, that's what I meant."

"How in heaven's name was I supposed to know that?" demanded Poole. "I can't read your mind."

Fitch barked: "Hey!"

Poole and I immediately quieted. Fitch was looking from one to the other of us. The expression on his face was one I imagine a lot of marriage counselors wear when they're in the middle of some spousal catfight.

The lieutenant looked at me pointedly. "I won't ask you again. If you want to keep on being allowed to sit in, I'm going to have to ask you to shut up."

"Sorry," I said for the second time. Fuming.

Fitch turned back to Poole. "So you went into the dead man's cottage?"

"I'm afraid so," Poole said.

"Did you touch anything?"

"I'm afraid so," Poole said.

"What?"

"My wine."

"You mean the bottle?"

Poole nodded. "While I was standing in the doorway, I couldn't tell for certain it was mine because the label side was to the floor. I wouldn't be absolutely sure unless I turned it over."

"So that's what you did? Turned it over?"

"Yes."

"You had to go right up next to the body to do that," said Fitch. "You didn't happen to notice anything else, did you?"

"Such as?"

"Signs of a struggle? Spots of blood? Anything out of the ordinary?"

Poole said sarcastically, "You mean, besides a corpse?"

Fitch's expression darkened. "Did you touch anything else?"

"No."

"You're sure of that?"

"Absolutely."

Fitch straightened in his chair, put his hands on his thighs, and seemed to consider what to do next. "I guess that's all for now, Mr. Poole," he said at last. "I'll probably want to talk to you some more later on."

"Is it all right if I get dressed?"

"Be my guest."

With more grace than I'd have expected, Poole lifted himself from the sofa and waddled off toward the bedroom, leaving Fitch and me alone. We heard the bedroom door closing.

Fitch turned to me with a curious look on his face. "What's the matter?" I asked.

He pointed his chin in the direction of Poole's bedroom and asked, "How much are you getting paid to baby-sit him?"

"Why do you ask?"

"Because," said Fitch, "whatever it is, it ain't enough."

AS FITCH AND I walked over to Paoletti's bungalow, we passed a couple of paramedics wheeling a sheet-wrapped body on a stretcher out of the front door. The deputy at the door— the same one who'd given me the suspicious look earlier— nodded when we entered. It was a deferential nod, not just to Fitch's position, it seemed, but as much to the man himself.

Fitch was a good cop, and I told myself I should just pull out of this business as soon as possible and let him deal with the situation.

Several evidence techs were still scurrying about inside the bungalow, checking out everything in the room. One was gathering fingerprints from the doorknob leading to the bathroom. Another carried a plastic bag with what I assumed was the tumbler Poole had referred to. A third stood with clipboard in hand, staring raptly at the papers attached, a look of tight-assed responsibility on his face.

Fitch introduced me to the tech in charge, a woman named Deana Simms. She was short and a bit stocky, her hair was jet black, and her expression said she'd done it all a thousand times before. She wore the feminine version of Fitch's sloppy-cop suit, a brown check. Her earrings were simple gold hoops.

"What have you got?" Fitch asked her.

"ME guesses he died around two-thirty this morning," Simms replied.

"Right around the time your friend Poole says he was chasing around after some chicken wings," Fitch said to me. "Maybe we should pump his stomach and see if there are really any in there."

"You're going to need a big pump," I said. I turned to Simms. "Do you know what kind of poison was used on the victim?"

Fitch and Simms both threw me the same suspicious-cop look. "Who said anything about poison?" Simms asked.

"I just figured—"

Damn Poole anyway. He never got around to explaining how he'd come to that particular conclusion. He'd also managed to leave that part out when he retold the story to Fitch. "No blood," I said, thinking quickly. "At least none that I can see, so that probably rules out a knife or gun. What's left?"

"He could have gotten clonked on the head by the bottle," Fitch suggested."

"Wouldn't a blow that hard break it?" Simms asked. "The bottle, I mean?"

"Not necessarily," I said. "Wine bottles are pretty strong. Actually, it was my employer who suggested poison. I guess I just assumed he knew what he was talking about."

"He does," Simms said. "No overt signs of violence on the body. Plus the ME happened to sniff the bottle. Bitter almonds."

"Cyanide?" Fitch asked.

Simms nodded. "So it would seem. Anything else I can do for you, Lieutenant? I haven't had any breakfast yet, and I'd kind of like to get done around here and go."

Fitch thanked her, and he and I made our exit. By now a few looky-loos had gathered, although the yellow crime scene tape was forcing them to keep their distance. I saw several people I recognized from the night before. Among them was Michael Gottberg, demanding to be let by, but the fact he was the head of NAMES carried zero weight with the deputies barring his way.

Peter Taylor stood by also. When he saw me, he waved. "Can you get me in there, Jack?"

Fitch said to me, "Isn't that Peter Taylor?"

"You know him?"

"We were in the same class at San Tomas. Didn't you know that?"

"I guess I forgot."

"What's he doing here?"

"This is his family's winery," I said. "Didn't you know that?"

"Obviously not."

We crossed to Peter, who looked just as surprised when he recognized Fitch as the lieutenant was to recognize him. They shook hands, not having crossed one another's paths since graduating from high school. Before they could get to reminiscing, though, I reminded Fitch what his colleague Deana Simms had said about wanting breakfast. I was hungry myself. Peter suggested we head over to the dining room, where he could also be brought up to speed on just what in the hell was going on.

As we were walking the path to the dining room, Peter asked Fitch, "Is Nicky Paoletti really dead?"

"He sure is," Fitch said.

"Murdered?"

"It looks like it."

"Do you know who did it?"

Fitch shook his head. "We will, though, soon enough."

"Peter," I said, "speaking of Nicky, you wouldn't happen to have a phone I could use, would you? I'd like to call my dad. I left the house in a rush this morning, and I kind of left him hanging. I'd like to let him know what's going on, just for the sake of his peace of mind."

"Sure." Peter indicated the outbuilding attached to the dining facility. "My office is open."

"I'll meet you guys in the kitchen," I said.

They waved me off and continued on their way.

Peter's office held a desk, some files, and the like. An old-style Catholic crucifix hung from the wall. I picked up the phone and punched up my home number.

Dad picked up on the second ring. I gave him a quick synopsis of the morning's events. The news that someone at Rancho Calzada had indeed been poisoned—and that the someone was Nicky Paoletti—took him aback.

"The case is in very good hands," I assured him. "Brad Fitch's."

"How's his shoulder?" asked Dad.

"Fine. I'm actually glad he's the one in charge, since I'll feel that much less guilty about keeping my nose out of it."

Dad chuckled sardonically. "You'll keep your nose out of it. Yeah, right."

"I'm not kidding."

"Whatever you say, Jack." He chuckled again. "By the way, Maggie called."

"When?"

"Not fifteen minutes ago. She said she was hoping to catch you before you took off for the day. You can't call her back at the office, though. She told me to tell you she's going to be up in Santa Maria with a client all day."

The pang I felt told me how much I was starting to miss her. I said good-bye to Dad and hung up.

On my way to the dining room, I was still thinking about Maggie, wondering idly what it would be like to have her at my beck and call all the time—as Poole had Carla at his. Of course, their relationship was entirely different. It had to be strictly business. No hanky-panky at all. That's when, unbidden, the image of a naked, rutting Augustus Poole popped into my mind. Underneath him in bed a couple of extremities stuck out, all that you could see of Carla Lubow.

And then I could hear the man himself, bellowing, making a giant fuss. Thankfully, as I hurried the last few steps into the dining room, the image of the naked Poole dissipated to whence it came.

The real, though now fully dressed Poole wasn't much better. At least the light gray tailored suit that he was wearing fit his corpulent form well. His shirt was white and his tie paisley—the type of tie that usually has a matching handkerchief sticking of the suit coat pocket, though none was there.

"Absolutely not!" he was shouting at Peter Taylor. "It is out of the question! You have already demonstrated to me that you cannot meet my needs!"

"Carla was next to Poole. She had on a dark green dress, several inches more above the knee than I would have expected, but I didn't mind. She kept making placating gestures to him, saying, "Everything's fine, Mr. Poole," over and over.

The rest of the group included Brad Fitch and Ted Taylor. Fitch was on the periphery. He'd pulled a chair out from one of the tables and sat on it backward, with his hands crossed in front of him atop the chair's back. He had a bemused expression on his face.

I joined the throng. Peter spotted me and said, "Jack, will you please tell him?"

"Tell him what?"

"That he's perfectly safe here."

I turned to Poole. "You're perfectly safe here." Back to Peter. "Anything else I can do?"

"Enough!" roared Poole. He shrugged his shoulders inside his coat and in a few seconds had regained his composure. "Mr. Donne?"

"Yes, Mr. Poole?"

"You will proceed with Miss Lubow to my bungalow. There you will give her any assistance she needs in packing my belongings. When she assures you she can complete the task without further assistance from you, you will fetch the car. We are going back to San Francisco."

"You can't!" cried Ted.

The mention of San Francisco brought Brad Fitch into the conversation. "I can't allow you to go anywhere, Mr. Poole," he said. "You're a material witness in a murder case. I can't just let you go blasting on back to Frisco whenever you want."

I'd swear Poole winced at the word "Frisco." But only for a moment. Then he drew himself up to his full height and fixed Fitch with a contemptuous stare. "Material witness?"

"At the very least," Fitch said. "If not an outright suspect."

"My dear Lieutenant Fitch, whatever college of criminology

did you graduate from? It seems clear to me—absolutely, perfectly clear, without a shadow of a doubt—that I was the intended *victim* in this matter. *Not* a suspect."

That stopped Fitch for a moment, and the Taylors too. It didn't stop Carla, though. She'd headed for the door around the time Fitch was labeling Poole a material witness, and was already several steps down the path back to the bungalows. On her way to pack Poole's bags, I supposed.

I came back to the conversation. Much as I might hate to admit it, Poole's assertion made sense to me. If somebody had meant to murder Nicky Paoletti, how would they know he was going to steal Poole's bottle of '47 Yquem? Plus, there were still those two previous incidents. Now I wasn't so sure they were coincidental.

Again: 90 percent of the time it's the obvious answer. And the obvious answer now was that the poison was meant for Augustus Poole.

"Mr. Poole," I said, "I promise you, Lieutenant Fitch is an extremely capable man." I shook my head, realizing that now *I* was talking like the fat fool. "If you are in danger, and I feel certain I can convince the lieutenant you are, he will gladly provide you with the highest level of security. Wouldn't that be satisfactory?"

"I will?" asked Fitch.

I nodded. All eyes turned to Poole. He waited for the proper dramatic moment, then uttered one word: "No."

Silence for a second or two, then all hell broke loose.

Both Taylors started chattering, assuring Poole yet again he would be entirely safe under their roof. Brad Fitch knocked over his chair in getting up, planted himself in Poole's face, and berated him for impugning the Santa Barbara County Sheriff's Department.

Finally Poole made a little dismissive motion with the fingers of an upraised hand, and everyone shut up again. It was amazing, really, the power the man could project. He gave the group an imperious sweep of his eyes. Finally he rested on me. "It's up to Mr. Donne."

"What's that supposed to mean?" Fitch asked.

"I'll stay, but only if I can have the constant presence of Mr. Donne. I have contracted for his services through Sunday, and I will stay only if that arrangement is honored. Mr. Donne will abide here at Rancho Calzada with me. Only then will I remain."

"I'm not staying here," I said.

"Nonsense," Poole said. "There is plenty of room. The unfortunate Mr. Paoletti's bungalow is now vacant, and I'm sure once the police are finished there we can get housekeeping to—"

"That's a crime scene," Fitch insisted. "Jack Donne's not moving in there, and neither is anybody else."

Poole threw Fitch a disdainful look. He pursed his lips, brought in a noisy lungful of air, blew it back out. "Very well. Of course, he could not possibly stay in my bungalow, and I'm afraid Miss Lubow would probably mind very much if he shared hers."

I broke in. "Trust me on this, Mr. Poole. She'd mind. Besides which, I don't *want* to stay here. I prefer to sleep in my own bed at night."

"Then," Poole said, "the solution is obvious, is it not?"

Ted, Peter, Fitch, and I all looked puzzled.

"It is?" I asked.

"Of course it is," said the huge man. "I shall stay at Mr. Donne's residence."

I spent half an hour trying to convince everyone that Augustus Poole's staying at my home was a lousy idea. Everyone was against me. Peter and Ted Taylor—as well as Joyce, who showed up about five minutes into the argument—wanted nothing more than for Poole to be happy and for the NAMES banquet to go on as planned. If that meant Poole would be insinuating himself on my household, so be it.

Brad Fitch, who also needed Poole to remain in the neighborhood, didn't want to dedicate any of his men to shepherding him around, and he thought I was just the guy to make sure the fat man didn't get into any more mischief. Poole himself had decided it was the most wonderful plan in the world, and nothing would convince him otherwise.

I probably could have worked it out with Fitch to stay at Rancho Calzada, even if it was in Paoletti's bungalow, but I'd taken my stand. Maybe it was stupid of me, but I can be a stubborn bastard at times. Plus everyone was leaning on me.

Long story short: I gave in.

I agreed to let Augustus Poole stay at Donne Vineyards through Sunday. Then I went off to figure out how to break the news to my father.

DAD WOULD HAVE none of it. "I don't even know this man," said my father. I was back on the phone in Peter's office near the dining room. "And given what I've heard about him, I'm not even happy he's here in the valley, much less in my house."

"*Our* house," I said.

"Whoever's. He'll probably eat us out of house and home. Besides, we don't have room."

"What's wrong with the guest room?"

"It's Gerry's room."

"Uncle Gerry lives in Santa Barbara."

"He might come for a visit. He does sometimes, you know."

"He won't."

"He *might*."

Before the conversation degenerated further, I decided to fall back on my father's sympathy. "I'm in a bind here, Dad. I don't want him in our house any more than you do, but there's really no choice."

Nothing from the other end of the line. My eye fell on the crucifix on the wall. Not that I'd ever been particularly religious, but right about then some divine help would have been welcome.

"Dad?"

"Oh, go ahead, bring him around. What the hell. It's only for two days, right?"

"Right." I allowed myself the little lie. It was only two full days, after all—Friday and Saturday. Plus large parts of Thursday and Sunday, but I figured I could smooth that out later.

"When are you bringing him home?" my father asked.

"I'm not sure. It depends on how soon Fitch will let him out of his sight. Although from what the lieutenant says, he'd just as soon let him out of his sight and keep him there."

"He sounds like a charming fellow."

"He has his moments. I'll make it up to you, Dad. Promise."

"How?"

"I'll think of something."

"You do that."

THE TAYLORS HAD fled to figure out who was going to be cooking the rest of the meals. I half expected them to cancel the whole thing, but it was going on as planned.

Poole, meanwhile, had attached himself to a group of newly arrived NAMES members, whom he regaled with the story of how he barely escaped with his life a few short hours ago. I hadn't seen Carla Lubow since she went off to pack while Poole was having his fit. I realized that no one had told her we weren't returning to San Francisco, so I walked back to Poole's bungalow. The air seemed ten degrees hotter than when I had ducked in to call my father. It sometimes does that in the Santa Ynez. You'll be thinking you've gotten away with a rare cool summer day, when pow, the real weather settles in.

I knocked on the door. She hadn't closed it properly, and it swung open. I stuck my head in and, in my most charming voice, said, "Ms. Lubow?"

The bathroom door slammed. "Who is it?" she asked from behind.

"Jack Donne."

"Oh." The bathroom door opened and out she came, Poole's shaving kit in hand. She showed me a weak smile. "I guess I'm just a little jumpy. I'm all finished here. When you didn't show up, I took care of everything myself."

She dropped the shaving kit in a suitcase and stepped toward me. "I'm sorry," she said.

"For what?"

"There wasn't really any reason to expect you to help me pack. That wasn't part of the arrangement. Also, I'm sorry Mr. Poole tried to order you around like that. He's just used to getting his way."

"I'm curious why you put up with it."

I'd thought she might have been thawing a bit, but the ice was back. Her body tensed—the sort of reaction you'd expect from somebody who wanted badly not to talk about something.

"Forgive me for asking," I said. "It's none of my business. We're just two people doing a job here. No reason we should know anything about each other." I pointed to the suitcase. "Are you ready to go?"

She nodded.

I closed the suitcase and picked it up off the bed. "Let's throw it in the trunk now," I said. "Then we won't have to come back."

I PROBABLY SHOULD have mentioned to her earlier in the conversation about the change in plans. But I realized that, much as I didn't want to be a detective again, I'd gotten a little charged up. The part of me I showed to the world didn't want anything to do with finding out who killed Niccolo Paoletti. But the part I kept to myself was more than a little curious. When that happens, I shift into cop mode. I wasn't quite the Jack Donne everyone knew and loved. My mind worked differently.

The way it worked was this: Given that no one knew Nicky Paoletti was going to steal Poole's Yquem—assuming that's how it got into Nicky's room—probably no one had killed him intentionally. Therefore, Poole was the target. This was what Poole had convinced me of, and the more I thought about it the more sense it made.

Ever since I'd gotten involved in the wine business, I'd heard about how everyone feared or hated Augustus Poole because of the immense power he wielded. Obviously, he'd hurt a lot of people—many of whom were here at Rancho Calzada or would be in the next day or so. One of them might have reason enough to kill him.

Then again, maybe it had been Carla.

Look at it this way. The folks whom Poole might have hurt didn't have to put up with him all the time. Carla did. And I'd had just enough experience in his presence to get a feeling for what that must be like. The constant irritation, the nagging, the supercilious bullshit, might finally have gotten to her.

So she'd what? Carried around some cyanide for who knows how long, just waiting for the right opportunity to present itself? That seemed a little far-fetched. But then, it was weird that *anyone* would be carrying around cyanide on the possibility you might find a use for it.

But suspect or not, I wanted to gauge Carla's reaction to finding out we were staying. She'd fled a little too quickly when Poole said we were leaving. So when she asked me if anyone had checked the schedule with the train station in Bakersfield, I said, in my best innocent voice, "Oh, didn't anyone tell you? We're not going back to San Francisco. Mr. Poole has decided to come home with me. My father and I will be putting him up."

For an instant, incomprehension flashed across her face. Then came a smile that—to my surprise—seemed real enough.

"That's wonderful," she said. "I'm sure Mr. Poole is very pleased. It's nice of you to take him in."

"Yes," I said. "Isn't it?"

. . .

POOLE'S SYCOPHANTS HAD deserted him to go off on a winery tour scheduled for all the NAMES members, so my obese charge had been seeking me out. I was just coming out of his bungalow when he caught up with me.

"Mr. Donne," he said, huffing and puffing from the exertion of going the length of the path at a brisk walk.

"Call me Jack," I said. I don't know why I said it. To see how he would react, I guess.

"I will do no such thing. We are business associates. I would never presume to call Miss Lubow, uh—"

She helped him out. "Carla."

"I would not call her Carla, nor would I expect her to call me by my given name—"

"Augustus," I said.

Such a dirty look he threw me. I stifled a grin. "Yes," he said. "Quite. I would not expect her to call me by my given name, nor would I expect you, so I will not use yours. If, over the course of our time together, you and Miss Lubow should reach a stage wherein you would feel comfortable using your Christian names with each other—"

At which point Poole exhibited a leer the likes of which I'd never seen. Evidently there was no middle ground in his book. Either you were on a last-name basis, or you were screwing. "If that were the case," he continued, "I would have no objection."

His gaze swung back and forth between Carla and me, a grandfatherly beaming. Augustus Poole, matchmaker. The thought was chilling.

Back to business. "Mr. Poole," I said, "do you have any idea who might have it in for you?"

"Wait a minute, Jack," said Brad Fitch. He was coming up

the path, rubbing a handkerchief over his forehead. "If Mr. Poole is going to give any information, I want to hear it first-hand." He whipped out a small pad of white paper and a pen that said OAKLAND ATHLETICS along the barrel.

Poole said to him, "If you are going to continue to pester me with inane questions instead of chasing after whoever is threatening me, as a proper policeman should, at least let us sit someplace comfortable."

I finished hauling Poole's luggage out to the Cadillac, then rejoined the others. The "someplace comfortable" we ended up was the living room of the Taylors' personal residence. We ran into Peter, who was still trying to scout up a new chef, and he told us it would be okay to use the room.

The room's decor was a fine example of the early Spanish influence brought into the twentieth century. The walls were white adobe. Dark wood moldings graced the ceiling. The main part of the room was carpeted in a rust-colored pile a couple of shades darker than the bricks that formed a two-foot-wide border around the edge. Several pieces of early Californian art graced the walls, including one huge painting of a group of people cheering for a young boy playing matador with a calf. There was other art too, including a Picasso lithograph and an African piece of a type Maggie McKenney had told me was called Shona, from Zaire, or Zambia, or Zimbabwe—one of those Z countries. Joyce Taylor had picked most of the stuff, I knew, and somehow she made it all work.

Light filtered in from two huge picture windows overlooking the vineyards. Poole moved to one of them as soon as we entered, stared out for fifteen or twenty seconds, then said, "Not bad, that view." Then he turned and surveyed the seating arrangements. Two dark brown leather sofas faced each other along the long axis of the room, with a giant stone fireplace at one end. He eyed first one sofa, then the other, then moved, quite gracefully, to an immense armchair sitting by itself in the corner. The chair, upholstered in a white, green, and rust Native American pattern, creaked under his weight. "I shall sit here," he announced. "That will be satisfactory, I trust."

It wasn't, really, as where he'd placed himself wasn't convenient to any of the other seating. Fitch grabbed a wooden chair and brought himself up near the great man. I ducked into a nearby den for a chair similar to Fitch's. When I sent Carla a questioning look, she shook her head. She moved to stand behind Poole's shoulder.

"All right, then, Lieutenant," said Poole. "What would you like to know?"

"You're going to make me ask again, aren't you?"

Poole said nothing until Fitch repeated his query as to who might want the fat man dead.

"Oh, that," Poole said. "Let me see. Just among those here now, or including those due for the banquet, or in the world at large?" He chuckled. "I suppose some of those whose reviews have been unsatisfactory might be angry at me. But such reviews are always deserved. And to consider that someone would want to kill me because of them is simply too far-fetched."

He leaned forward conspiratorially. I found myself leaning with him. Fitch rolled his eyes.

"No," Poole said, in a voice barely above a whisper.

"Could you speak up, please?" asked Fitch.

"This is a moment of high drama. I am about to reveal who I think is trying to murder me."

"Mr. Poole?" I said.

"Yes?"

"The drama might be minimized if no one can hear what you're saying."

He sat back again, seeming to consider this. "Good point,

Mr. Donne. You do have a head on your shoulders after all."

"Please," Fitch said wearily. "Can we just get on with it? Who do you think would want to kill you?"

"It is"—Poole puffed out his chest, slowly swiveled his head around to encompass all present—"It is someone from my past."

Fitch looked at me. I looked right back at him. Both of us turned to Carla. She shrugged. "That's it?" Fitch asked. "Someone from your past? *Who* from your past? Give me a name. Give me a description. Give me something to go on."

"That's all I feel certain of," said Poole. "It should be enough." He seemed very pleased with himself. "It is someone from my past, I'm sure. Probably someone I don't even remember. Some long-dead perceived insult, perhaps, or an affair of the heart when I was younger. *Much* younger. Someone I probably don't even remember is coming after me with runaway cars and bullets and poisoned sauternes. It would all be very romantic if it weren't so very frightful."

Fitch slammed shut his notebook. I don't know how he got so much noise out of a ninety-nine-cent pad, but he did.

"Jack," he said, "whatever you do, don't let this guy out of your sight. There's something going on here I don't get, but I'm going to find out what it is."

Poole couldn't resist. "There is probably a considerable amount that you don't 'get,' Lieutenant. But I shall give you all the assistance I can. Though I wonder if a backwoods police force like yours can—"

"What kind of police force?"

"Backwoods," repeated Poole.

Fitch looked ready to slug him. "We do the best we can here in these 'backwoods,' and usually that's just fine. So watch yourself, Mr. Poole. Or you're going to end up in jail."

That got to him. The color drained from Poole's face, and

with a face like his, that was a lot of color. "Jail?" He sounded a little like a frightened child.

"Ever been in jail, Mr. Poole?" asked Fitch. "No? I didn't think so."

Poole may have been getting my goat, but he was getting Fitch's whole herd. It was time to step in. "Look," I said, "everybody should just make nice now. We all have the same purpose here, don't we? We find out who poisoned Mr. Poole's wine, all our problems are solved."

Silence for a few seconds. "I will if he will," said Poole, indicating Fitch.

"I will if he will," said Fitch. "But, Jack?"

"Yeah?"

"I still don't want you to let him out of your sight. Of course, big as he is, that shouldn't be difficult."

Before either Poole or Carla could get out the protests they were formulating, Fitch strode out of the room. I looked at Poole. "Someone from your past? Is that the best you could do?"

"Trust me, Mr. Donne. I feel very strongly about this. And now, shall we be off?"

"Off?" I said. "Off where?"

"Off to find whoever is trying to kill me. Together, I believe the two of us can track him—or her—down."

"You're not seriously thinking about playing detective, are you?"

"It seems to me a capital idea. Come, Miss Lubow, Mr. Donne. Let us also find something edible. I trust that the unfortunate death of Mr. Paoletti, ill-mannered as he was, has not exhausted the reserves of decent chefs in this fine town."

He extracted his girth from the chair and waddled out of the room. Carla Lubow followed close behind. I was starting to get used to bringing up the rear.

itch had gone off to track down some more of last night's guests. Poole, meanwhile, had gotten it into his head that the arrangements for the banquet probably weren't suitable, so he and Carla embarked on a grand tour of the banquet room. I managed to convince him that he wasn't in any danger if I were just one room away while he completed his important task.

I met up with Peter Taylor in the kitchen. I was again struck by how agitated he seemed, not at all the calm, collected Peter I'd known for many years. For a moment I entertained the thought that *he* was the killer. It seemed a stupid thought, and I gave it the short shrift it deserved.

Then I found out why Peter was so upset. "My father's having a fit," he said. "What with Paoletti dead, he doesn't have a proper chef for Saturday night's dinner, and—"

I held up a hand. "Peter?"

"Yes?"

"Doesn't it strike you as odd that, first of all, you're going ahead with this dinner, and second, that everyone seems to be so blasé about Nicky Paoletti getting knocked off?"

Peter sighed. "Yeah, it does. But I keep seeing how worried Dad is. He's wanted into NAMES for a long, long time. And now to see his chance slipping away . . ." He sighed again. "Dad really didn't know Paoletti that well. None of us did."

"It just seems sort of macabre to me."

A shrug. "They're an odd group, these—"

"Foodies?"

He frowned. "I'm glad my father wasn't around to hear you say that. In any case, they are kind of strange. Mom and I've always indulged Dad about his wanting to join, even though— and if you tell him I said it, I'll say you're full of crap—we think they're a bunch of lunatics. Harmless, but lunatics nonetheless."

"One of them probably isn't so harmless."

"You think someone in NAMES killed Paoletti?"

"There were enough of them around last night, and I'm positive Brad Fitch is going to treat some of them as suspects. Including you."

"*Me?*"

"You were on the premises. Your parents too. Don't be surprised if the questions start getting a lot more personal if this thing doesn't get cleared up soon."

"Oh." It sounded like there might be a lot going on behind that single word, but Peter failed to expand.

One of the kitchen help walked by, a young Hispanic man carrying a tray of unbaked rolls. He whistled as he worked, some mariachi-sounding tune. I watched him place the tray on a counter and disappear through the swinging door to the dining room.

I turned back to Peter. "Come on, out with it. We've known each other a long time. Whatever you're hiding, Fitch is going to find out whether you tell me or not. It'll look better if he doesn't have to dig."

Peter sighed. "It was eight years ago. We'd just released the best cabernet sauvignon we'd ever made, up to that time. We've always been proud of our cabs, but this was really something special."

He paused as the young Hispanic man came back into the kitchen, accompanied by a blondish girl of about seventeen. Peter gave them some instructions concerning table settings in what I took to be reasonable Spanish, and sent them on their way.

He turned back to me. "Poole slammed it. Not just once, but in two separate articles. One in the *San Francisco Chronicle*, in a guest column in a food section, and the other in his damned newsletter."

"*Pooled Knowledge?*"

Peter nodded. "Is that a stupid name or what? Anyway, what really got Dad was not so much that Poole bad-rapped the wine. Which he did, by the way, comparing it with some swill that wasn't even in the same ballpark. But what galled Dad was that he also took us to task for having the presumption to speak highly of the wine. Dad had been talking it up, and evidently word got back to Poole, who took it on himself to punish him for pushing his own product." He paused. "Goddammit, Jack, my father was proud of that cab. All he did was tell somebody from the local press that. You know these local papers, they're always looking for things that make the valley look good."

"Nothing wrong with that."

"Yeah, but you know the vineyards around here. Although not everyone will admit it, a lot of them have this thing about Napa. They all feel that everybody outside of the state thinks of up north as the whole California wine industry. So the local guy who wrote the article said our cab compared to the very best from Napa, even though Dad hadn't said a word to that effect. Somehow Poole got hold of the article and decided to pick on us."

"I remember the wine," I said. "It still sold pretty well, didn't it? I think my father and I cellared a whole case."

"It did okay," Peter said. "But it should have done great. That it didn't is something Dad has always blamed on Poole."

"Blame him enough to want to do something about it?"

"He was pretty pissed off. He made some harsh statements."

"Such as?"

"The one I remember is that he would have liked to slit Poole open and let the vultures eat his guts."

"Your father said that?"

"See? That was my reaction too. Dad's the most civilized guy I know. He never says a bad word about anybody. But this really hit him where he lived."

"Did he get over it?" I asked.

Peter shrugged. "More or less. The wine got some solid reviews—the *Spectator* gave it a 91—but somehow those two negative ones of Poole's took the shine off it." He shook his head. "Of course, Dad wouldn't ever do anything about it. Except he won't let anything with Poole's writing in it into the house. Mom has to go read *Bon Apetit* over at a friend's."

"How does she feel about all this? Your mom, I mean?"

"She was angry too—at least at first. But she got over it. Rancho Calzada—the place, not the grapes—is her life. She doesn't have nearly as much emotional investment in the wines."

"So with your father feeling the way he does, how's he dealing with Poole being the guest speaker at the very banquet intended to get him into NAMES?"

"He's living with it. Poole was picked long before we got the bid to host the banquet. Dad almost withdrew when he found out, but he wants to get into NAMES more than anything. Besides, this thing with the bad reviews was eight years ago, and . . . Dad's tolerating it. He's putting up a good front."

"Poole probably doesn't even remember the damn review," I said. "So what about you?"

"What about me?"

"How do you feel about him?"

Peter tugged on his lower lip while he thought about that. "He's obviously an asshole. But I can put up with him for four days. I've dealt with a lot of assholes in my time." He smiled. "Why? Do you think I had something to do with Nicky's murder?"

"No," I said. "But Fitch might. And even if he doesn't, he's paid to act as if he does. I just wanted to introduce you to the possibility that you might seem to be under suspicion."

I stretched. "I suppose it's time for me to get back to the great man himself. What are you going to be up to today?"

"Mostly finding someone to cook Saturday night. Know anybody?"

I shook my head. "Maybe I can get a recommendation from Poole."

Peter laughed, although it seemed a little uncomfortable. "Just don't tell Dad where it came from."

"I won't." I headed for the dining room, thinking about how it was impossible to consider Peter Taylor a killer. Then again, you wouldn't have thought it of the man who'd done in Perry Cole, either, a few months back. Murder's funny that way.

AUGUSTUS POOLE RAISED an eyebrow as I approached. "Hmf," he said. "I'm lucky I wasn't slaughtered where I stood while you were gallivanting around."

"As are we all, Mr. Poole," I said. "Lucky, I mean. I too would be sad if you were to meet your demise. There's my fat fee to think of. If you were to die, I might never get it."

"If I were to die, you wouldn't have earned it, would you?"

"Good point."

"Mr. Donne," Carla said. "Mr. Poole would like some breakfast."

"So be it," I said.

We went outside, where it seemed another several degrees hotter, and escaped into the quickly air-conditioned comfort of Uncle Gerry's Seville. I started the car and drove off, headed for—where?

I couldn't think of a restaurant in the immediate area that would assuage Poole's need for sustenance. Not that we don't have our share of decent restaurants in the valley, but most of them are open only for lunch and dinner. Those that serve breakfast are down toward Santa Barbara, farther than I wanted to drive with my two charges. I grinned, picturing Poole jammed into a booth at Esau's, a fabulous dive in downtown SB. He wouldn't know what to make of it. And if he gave them any shit, they'd just give it right back.

I briefly considered dumping them at the local Denny's and coming back to pick up the pieces later, but that would never do. People knew me around these parts. I'd never be forgiven.

Then it hit me. Sooner or later Dad would have to meet Poole. Why not bring him over now, get it over with, and have Dad rustle up some food? Poole would probably hate it, and my father would be angry at me. But he already was anyway. Maybe I could dump Poole off at home, have him tour the vineyards or something, and get some decent work done on the investigation.

Then I remembered: It wasn't my investigation.

Yes, I was playing private detective again, but no, it wasn't as some sort of police adjunct in the affair of Niccolo Paoletti's death. It was as bodyguard to Augustus Poole. And what better way to guard his rather sizable body than to haul it off to someplace relatively isolated, where, I hoped, the supposed murderer wouldn't think to look for him?

"Mr. Poole," I said, "how about a nice home-cooked meal?"

He was sitting beside me in the front passenger seat, straining the seat and shoulder belts to their utmost. It was like driving alongside Buddha. I awaited the announcement that home cooking was an abhorrent phenomenon, to be suffered only by the sweating masses. "And in whose home would this be?"

"Mine. My father's not a half-bad chef." I almost said the word "cook" but caught myself in time.

Oh, that Augustus Poole—always full of surprises. "A splendid idea, sir. A home-cooked meal would be just the thing to soothe my troubled soul after the recent unpleasantnesses. Proceed at once!"

I chanced a glance at him. His expression, too, was Buddha-like. I had no idea what he was thinking.

"Do you mean it?" I asked, returning my attention to the road. "This isn't just more of your famous sarcasm, is it?"

"I assure you I mean it. And I also assure you that when you are the victim of my sarcasm, you will know it. Proceed to your residence, and make it snappy. We shall eat, and then we shall plan our strategy."

One more quick look over. He just sat there with a little self-satisfied smile. And I couldn't help the strangest feeling that—dear God—Augustus Poole was actually starting to like me.

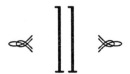

fter showing Poole to the guest room and dropping off his bags, I led Poole and Carla outside to track down Dad. He was propelling himself via quad cane down the rows of our chardonnay grapes, pausing now and then to examine the fruit.

"And this must be the elder Mr. Donne?" Poole said. "I am Augustus Poole."

My father somewhat reluctantly held out his hand. It hovered there in the sunlight for five or six seconds, until Carla rushed up and took it. Dad looked at me, puzzled.

"Mr. Poole doesn't like to shake hands," I said. "It's nothing personal. I'm sure he'll explain it to you sometime."

"Perhaps," Poole said. "But for now, let us proceed to breakfast."

We proceeded. It's amazing watching my father in the kitchen, moving around like a hobbled whirlwind. In no time, he whipped up some of his renowned shirred eggs with secret spices, a secret because they were different each time he made them, whatever was handy seeming to go in. The eggs were accompanied by slices of Virginia ham, quickly fried in oil with just a dash of Madeira. I rummaged around and came up with a box of Bisquick that I managed to camouflage while Poole was spouting off about his most recent Far East gastronomic adventure. I made coffee, Dad squeezed some oranges and fried some potatoes and onions, and there it was—home-cooked breakfast.

We put some flowers on the kitchen table and broke out the semi-good tablecloth. I feared for the chair Poole sat in, but it held. He tucked a napkin under his chin, dipped a fork into his eggs—and pronounced them delicious.

This decision was followed by similar pronouncements about the ham, the potatoes, even the orange juice. Only the biscuits met with disapproval. Poole pronounced them "serviceable, but with a bland commercial aftertaste."

Carla seemed to be enjoying herself too, while Dad and I kept exchanging glances, waiting for the drop of another shoe. But Poole wasn't fooling. After he'd finished eating, he patted his napkin daintily to his mouth and emitted one of the more musical belches I've heard.

He looked sheepish for a moment, then excused himself. "Mr. Donne," he said, carefully refolding his napkin and placing it on his plate. "Mr. Donne, Mr. Donne, Mr. Donne."

"Which one?" Dad and I asked at the same time.

"The elder," Poole said. "Mr. Donne, have you ever considered becoming a professional chef?"

"Never," Dad said.

"Perhaps you should. I enjoyed this meal more than any I've had in a week. Good old-fashioned American cooking, that's the stuff." He paused. "You wouldn't happen to know how to prepare terrapin Maryland, would you?"

"I'm afraid our terrapin crop's been a little scant this year," Dad said.

Poole tented his fingers. "Think about it. There aren't

enough good chefs in the world, much less in California." He closed his eyes, evidently a requirement for proper oratory. "Oh, there are pretenders, like our late friend Mr. Paoletti, who possess a certain flair, a certain je ne sais quoi. But true culinary genius, the ability to make brilliance with ordinary ingredients—that is indeed rare." His eyes opened, and he looked directly at my father. "Just work on your biscuits."

"I made the biscuits," I admitted.

"I see," Poole said. He shrugged, the barest lifting of his shoulders. "Well, Mr. Donne the younger, you have other talents, eh? Besides cooking? For example, perhaps it has occurred to you how we are going to find out who's trying to kill me without placing Miss Lubow or myself into any further peril?"

"I think I'll go outside," Dad said. "Just leave the dishes. I'll get to them in a little while." He got up and hobbled off down the hallway.

Poole said to me, "So?"

"So," I said, trying to ignore the feeling that what I was about to say would be breath wasted. "We sit tight. I guard your body. We stay out of harm's way until Sunday, Lieutenant Fitch catches the bad guy, and that's that."

"I think that's a good idea, Mr. Poole," Carla said. "Why don't you just stay here and explore the vineyards? I'll keep you company with Mr. Donne. I'm sure the three of us can find plenty to do."

Poole shook his head. "Unfortunately, I don't agree with either of you. Someone wishes to kill me. We are going to find out who it is. Anyone who doesn't want to do so can consider himself or herself fired."

Carla tried to dissuade Poole a few more times, but to no avail. It was clear she wasn't afraid of being fired, though. I found that out when Poole got up to go to the bathroom, and I asked her about it."

"He's fired me seven times I can think of," she said. "And I've quit at least five more. It's never for real, though. He needs me, and he knows it. I'm good at what I do."

I sensed she may have been thawing a little again, but there was still a lot of cold. "He knows that all of his projects and his publications are really my responsibility," she went on. "All the details, all the planning—he knows he's not going to find anyone else to do as good a job and put up with his foolishness."

"But what do you get in return?"

"Mr. Donne!"

It was Poole, sounding as if he was still in the guest bathroom. I walked out of the kitchen and down the hall, then stood a respectable distance from the bathroom door. "Yes, Mr. Poole?"

"Do you have any softer tissue?"

"Tissue?"

"Must I be vulgar? All right, then—toilet paper. What you have here is rather rough."

Perhaps it was. Dad and I had long ago taken to buying the kind made of recycled material—our way of giving back to the land and all. "Let me check."

I explored the cabinet where we keep our paper goods. Behind the twenty-four-pack of recycled paper, I found one solitary roll of Charmin we'd neglected to use up. I took it back to the bathroom. "Mr. Poole?"

"Yes?"

"I found a roll of something softer."

"Please place it on the floor outside the door. So I can—"

"I understand." I put the toilet paper on the floor and stepped away. "It's here."

After a few seconds his pudgy hand poked out, felt around, found the roll of paper, and withdrew. The door slammed shut. I tried not to think about what was happening on the other side.

I went back to Carla, who'd poured herself another cup of coffee. "I was about to ask you what you got out of your position with Poole," I said, resuming my seat. "Before we were interrupted."

"I get to travel," she said. "Quite a lot. All expenses paid. I also have a very good salary. And I get to meet interesting people."

"Like me?"

A bit of a challenging look. "All sorts. A lot of them are pompous, obnoxious jerks, but some of them are very interesting. Nicky Paoletti, for example. It's too bad he's dead."

I was about to follow up on that when I heard the toilet flush and the bathroom door opening. Poole returned to the kitchen. In his hand he held the roll of Charmin. "If you would be so kind, Mr. Donne," he said, giving it to me, "I would like you to put this somewhere safe. I'll probably need it again, and I don't want to find that someone else has used it up. You understand, of course."

I understood. I understood that the next three days were probably going to be an absolute living hell.

BY THE TIME we were ready to get on the road, it was nearly noon. Poole insisted that we follow the tour the NAMES members were on and track them down, so we could take them aside one by one and find out what they knew about events of the night before. I tried to point out that Brad Fitch would be questioning everyone himself, and that he was probably a lot better at it than we could be.

Outside it was even hotter than before. According to our outdoor thermometer, it was ninety-eight. On our way out we ran into my father, who was snipping a few flowers for the house. Poole asked him what was for dinner.

Dad said, "I don't know. We don't always plan dinner around here. Maybe some steaks or chops. Although—"

He caught my eye and winked. "We haven't been to Pea Soup Anderson's in a while, over in Buellton. Jack and I usually like to go a couple times a week, don't we, Jack? Best split pea soup in the world."

Poole obviously had heard of the famous tourist-trap greasy spoon, whose signs were posted up and down along U.S. 101 for hundreds of miles in both directions. His expression reflected a worse horror than any he'd felt about someone being out to kill him.

"That's what we ought to do," Dad said. "Pea Soup Anderson's. My treat." He placed his clippers on a railing, turned, and went back inside with his flowers.

Poole stood there stunned. I gave his shoulder a little push. He didn't even notice I'd taken the liberty of touching him. "Come on, Mr. Poole," I said. "The bad guys await."

As we ambled toward the car, Poole uttered, "I trust he was joking."

"Dad?" I smiled an evil smile. "That's the problem. You never know when he's kidding and when he isn't."

Poole groaned.

ccording to the itinerary, the NAMES people were supposed to be at Goodyear Vineyards around this time. Goodyear lies a couple of miles northwest of Highway 154, amid some gentle hills overlooking a broad, flat valley, only fifteen minutes or so from my home in San Tomas. When we arrived, no one was there but employees and a carload of four old ladies from Oregon. I assumed the ladies were there for a tour, although from the amount of wine stacked in the back of their Volvo wagon, maybe they just intended to grab a few more cases and run.

I've known Jim and Bess Goodyear since I was a kid. They're nice folks, and they make some nice, mid-priced table wines. They've earned enough money over the years to have expanded, but they've kept the winery fairly small, satisfied to put out a decent product at a fair price.

Jim happened to be out front when we arrived. "Hey, Jack!" he called when he saw me. "What's up?"

"What's up with you, Jim? Where's all the NAMES big-wigs?"

"Not here yet. I got a call—they're running behind. Apparently because of the police questioning everybody. Helluva thing that happened last night, wasn't it?"

"Helluva thing."

"I only met Nicky Paoletti one time, but—" He gulped. "Holy cow. Is that who I think it is getting out of your car?"

I followed his gaze, and we watched Augustus Poole extract himself from the Seville. Eventually his full bulk made it into the open air, accompanied by several grunts.

Poole lumbered over to us, with Carla in his wake. Jim held out a hand, and once again Carla knew what to do. Jim's reaction was much as my father's, clutching Carla's fingers while realizing that Poole had just refused his handshake. I'd finally figured out that this was one of the regular duties for which she was so well paid.

"Mr. Poole, a pleasure to meet you," Jim said when he'd regained his composure.

"Likewise, I'm sure, Mr.—?"

I jumped in. "This is Jim Goodyear, Mr. Poole. He's the owner."

"Of course," Poole said. He swept his arm around to encompass the vineyard. "Pleasant place you have here. I don't believe I've ever had the opportunity to sample your wares. Perhaps I can do so after we pose some questions to some—some suspects, would it be correct to say, Mr. Donne?"

"Maybe you can go do some sampling now, because the suspects aren't here yet. Jim has just informed me that they've been delayed. It seems Lieutenant Fitch is doing some questioning of his own."

"Is he?" Poole said. "How rude of him. I'm sure his questions are quite pedestrian and pointless. Oh well, I shall get my chance when they arrive. Did you mention sampling, Mr. Goodyear?"

"Right this way," said Jim.

The two of them walked off toward a redbrick building. They'd gone about ten yards down the path when Jim turned, caught my eye, and raised his eyebrows. I shrugged, which was enough to let him know I knew why he was giving me the look.

It was this: Not three years before, Poole had given one of the Goodyears' chards a scathing review. I didn't remember the details, but the word "vinegar" was prominent. The review was entirely undeserved. I didn't think the wine was among Goodyear's best, but it was better than the review would have had Poole's readers believe.

But Jim Goodyear, unlike Ted Taylor, hadn't given a damn. Jim knew his wine was good, his colleagues knew, and his regular customers knew, and that was all that mattered. He didn't hold a grudge. I could probably strike him off my list of suspects—not that he was on it in the first place.

But what had just happened pointed out two things to me. First, that the epicurean world was going to be full of people who would have reason to hate Augustus Poole. At one time or another, he'd said bad things about almost every winery we'd driven past in the last day, as well as several others around the world I could think of off the top of my head. And Poole didn't only deal with wine. He'd no doubt pissed off loads of restaurants too. Who else? Cooking schools? Food publishers? Entire cities, even? I recalled a column of his describing a trip to Sacramento, where he claimed he couldn't find a decent bite to eat in the whole city. Now, Sacramento may not be the culinary capital of the planet, but I've had some perfectly good meals there.

Maybe that was it. Maybe the Sacramento City Council had hired a hit man to put cyanide in Poole's sauternes.

The second thing I realized was that Poole didn't remember stuff he'd written as recently as three years before. This was what had brought on Jim Goodyear's funny look. Not that you'd expect Poole to remember every word he'd ever written, but he obviously thought he'd never tasted Goodyear's chard. And if he didn't remember this, did he remember Ted Taylor's wine, eight years before? Or any of the other people, products, and establishments he'd put down?

It would be ironic if whoever was after Poole—and I realized at that moment I was absolutely sure that Paoletti had been an unlucky innocent bystander—was after him for something Poole had no recollection of.

When Jim and Poole went off, Carla had headed back to the Seville. She was sitting in the driver's seat, with the doors and windows closed. I walked up and motioned for her to roll down the window. "Any particular reason you're here?" I asked.

"I was hot. I thought you might have left the key and I could turn on the air-conditioning."

"I'm sure it's air-conditioned inside the winery. It stays cool in there all the time."

"I didn't want to go in with them just yet."

"Oh?"

She considered her answer. "Sometimes I need to be by myself for a few minutes. To remind myself what I'm getting out of this position. Then I'm fine."

It made sense—sort of. Getting sick of Poole was something anyone could do in a relatively short time. But he'd been on his best behavior since the toilet paper incident. If Carla needed a breather from him, this didn't seem a logical time.

The car door opened, and she stepped out, exposing enough thigh to distract me momentarily. She knew I'd seen her, so maybe she did it on purpose. Maybe she knew she was acting funny and wanted to shift my attention. If that was the case, she did a fine job.

She shut the door and stood close to me. I had the briefest urge to kiss her, but the impulse passed. Instead of doing something stupid, I took her arm and guided her toward the winery. On the way, I brought up the subject of Poole's not remembering that he'd reviewed—and slammed—Goodyear's wine.

"He does that," Carla said. "Sometimes it's embarrassing. I have to think fast when he doesn't remember somebody he's written poorly of. Or highly of, for that matter. Although why I bother trying to smooth things over, I don't know. He certainly doesn't care. All he cares about are enjoying his food and wine, and letting as many people as possible know about his opinions. None of it's ever personal."

"What happens when people feel hurt?"

"He's incapable of thinking in those terms. It's all about the food, about the wine, about the experience. The people don't matter."

As we were nearing the relative dimness of the winery building, we stopped, hearing the loud chatter of gravel on an automobile undercarriage. Two big vans pulled into the lot, the kind that hold about a dozen people apiece. A few seconds later people began to get out. I spotted the man from New York and the woman from Miami with whom I'd shared a table the night before, and as I walked over to their van, I nodded to both. Each said, "Good afternoon, Jack," and I replied noncommittally, since I still had no clue what their names were.

Ted and Joyce Taylor were the last to emerge from the second van. Ted had on a blue shirt with little Polynesian patterns, over khaki slacks and a new-looking pair of deck shoes. Joyce's dress was white and sleeveless. The other NAMES visitors were a mixed bag, sartorially speaking. Some wore sandals, shorts, and T-shirts advertising various wineries and restaurants. A few had on more expensive sportswear. One old guy wore a dark blue suit—wool, it appeared—with a red tie and pocket hankie. He looked as cool as a cucumber. Some people can do that, but not me. If I wear a dark suit on a hot day, I start to *smell* like a cucumber.

Ted drew me aside. "Your friend Lieutenant Fitch is quite a character."

I made a gesture to include the assembled masses. "You want to join up with *these* people, and you call Fitch a character?"

"But he's so—so dogged. Each and every one of us that was there last night got the third degree. What did we see, what did we hear, was anyone acting suspicious. It got awfully tedious after a while."

"Did he find out anything?"

"I don't know," Ted said. "Of course, I was only in on my own interrogation—well, Joyce's too, since he did us together. But I was also able to watch when he talked to some of the others. Every once in a while he'd get this expression on his face, like someone had said something important, and he'd write it down in his little book. It was a bit intimidating. I wondered if he was condensing what I said, whether it really reflected my words, or whether down the line I'd be accused of saying something I hadn't."

"Brad's a good cop," I said. "He'll actually remember most of it. The book is just backup. In fact, sometimes I think it's just a prop. To make him look more like a detective." I paused. "Ted, forgive me for this, but did he ask you if you might be harboring a grudge against Poole?"

For a second I thought he was going to get mad at me, until he realized the question came from a sincere desire to help. "I suppose you know about that incident several years ago?"

"Peter told me about it this morning."

Ted looked over near the vans, where Joyce and Sam Cardenas, the winemaker at Rancho Calzada, were trying to corral the NAMES folks for the walk into the Goodyears' winery. Several had strayed—one was halfway to the vines already. Like a bunch of unruly kids.

Ted said, "Fitch quizzed me about that. Joyce too. His interested was piqued, but I didn't get the feeling he thought that made me a real suspect. That's what I'd be, isn't it?"

I nodded. "From what I hear, though, nearly everyone could be a suspect."

He sighed. "I suppose. Poole has slammed just about everybody here at one time or another. But—and I hate to admit this, because he can be such an obnoxious character—he's as lavish with his praise as with his carping. It all balances out after a while." He fixed me with his eyes. "Do *you* suspect me, Jack?"

"Of course not." I smiled. "I know how much you want to be in NAMES. Why would you screw up your chances by knocking off Poole?"

Joyce and Sam had more us less gotten the group in order, and they'd proceeded into the main building, Ted and I following. It was dim in the welcoming room, the place set up much like all those in the wineries that give tours on a regular basis. The walls held frames with various awards and glowing reviews achieved by Goodyear Vineyards. There were a couple of autographed pictures of famous people in the company of Jim Goodyear, and some with his wife Bess. The prize was a big frame holding a letter and photo—Ronald Reagan, from his presidential days. The letter thanked Jim for supplying several cases of wine for the 1984 inauguration. Jim always made sure anyone who visited had a chance to see this artifact.

Off to one side was a counter at which you could purchase the vineyard's product. Jim was running a NAMES gathering special on his goods—15 percent off the regular price, 20 percent off case lots. Tempting, to say the least. It had certainly tempted the little old ladies from Oregon, who'd just finished buying two cases, as well as some assorted bottles. One of Jim's workers came out with a hand truck, loaded them up, and helped them out the door with their stash. As they left I overheard one of them suggesting they go next to "that Donne place." I thought of telling them we were open only on weekends, then decided to hell with it. Good luck, Dad.

The young woman working the counter told us that Jim would show up soon to lead everyone on a "deluxe personal tour." He was still with Mr. Poole, she added, who she indicated seemed very impressed with the winery.

I heard several "oohs" and "aahs" at the mention of Poole's name—and also one "ugh," which I wished I'd been able to figure out who'd uttered. The NAMESies—which is how I found myself thinking of them—apparently hadn't known he was going to be there. I studied several faces, trying to gauge expressions, looking for a negative reaction.

Then I heard Poole, before I actually saw him. "I'm rather disappointed in that '94 of yours," came his voice from outside the door leading into the tasting room. "To me, it has a slightly floral undertaste that I'd prefer wasn't there. There shouldn't be any undertaste at all. The floral quality should simply be melded with the overall essence."

The essence of what? I wanted to know. Jim Goodyear, though, seemed not to care. He was nodding dutifully, but he had a tiny smile on that told me he took little of Poole's criticism seriously. The NAMESies, on the other hand, were duly impressed, many of them nodding with knowing looks.

"Ah. Hullo, everyone," Poole said. "It's good to see you all." His expression spoke elsewise, but no one seemed to mind. "I'm glad to have you all here in one place. I have something to say."

Carla had positioned herself at the wall behind Poole. I watched her checking out the crowd; she reminded me of a Secret Service agent. Each face got just the briefest look—scanned, recorded, filed away. Mine got the same brief look, and the expression on her face held no sign we'd just spent the last several hours together. It was as if she didn't know me at all.

Poole went on. "It's clear someone is out to kill me. It pains me to say this, as I have always been as fair and just and good a critic as I know how. But the evidence is overwhelming."

He indicated me. "Some of you know that I have contracted with Mr. Donne here. He is acting as my bodyguard, and he is doing a fine job of it. But a reactive approach is not enough. We must find out who is behind this!"

It seemed like he was awaiting applause. None came, fortunately. He went on.

"Since we cannot count on adequate assistance from the authorities, it has become clear to me that I must solve this crime myself. Much as I have unlocked the mysteries of the epicurean world, much as I have delved into the complexities of fine wine to extract the truth, I will find out who is behind this terrible crime and bring him to justice."

"Or her," I contributed.

"Um. Mr. Poole?"

It was the guy from New York. "Mr. Poole, not to question your abilities, of course, but how are you going to do this?"

Poole pursed his lips, hauled in a bunch of air, and spit it back out. "I suppose that is a fair question. I shall start by questioning all those present here now, and—"

"Mr. Poole!"

Everyone turned to see who had spoken. It was a tall, slim woman in her late forties. Her hair was gray—not old-person gray, but the gray of someone whose hair has turned at a young age and who doesn't care. She was attractive enough, though a bit severe for my tastes. She wore a pale blue cotton blouse. That was all I could see of her attire; the rest was hidden by those around her. She stood near the front of the group. I perked up, determined to discover if her voice had been the one that had uttered that "ugh" from before.

After a suitable dramatic pause, Poole said, "Ms. Forsythe?"

"I wouldn't want to be the one to burst your bubble, Mr. Poole," she said, "but the police seem to have been very thorough with their investigation. We have been questioned up the yin-yang, and I think I speak for all of us when I say it's quite enough. I don't think another round of fact-finding by, let's be frank, a rank amateur is going to do any good."

Carla Lubow bristled. She took two steps away from the wall and seemed about ready to run through the crowd and punch the woman's lights out. Poole said, "Ms. Forsythe, I have no bubble to burst. It irritates me that you would feel that way."

"It irritates me that our tour is to be interrupted by your megalomaniacal quest."

"Excuse me?"

"Megalomaniacal. It means—"

"I know what the word means. And it irritates *me* that you would hang that appellation on me. Perhaps I have not had the experience of an Inspector Maigret, a Hercule Poirot—"

"A Jessica Fletcher," I muttered.

"—but I do know *people*. I know how to get to the truth. In any event, you needn't worry about your precious tour. It shan't be interrupted. It may begin immediately. I shall merely take each of you NAMES members aside, one by one, for a few minutes of questioning. All others will proceed on their tour, at this vineyard and at the ones to follow later this afternoon."

Ms. Forsythe seemed to realize it was pointless to argue any further, expecially since everyone else was nodding and smiling as if this new game were part of the festivities. "Whatever you say."

"Then shall we proceed? One of you will come with Mr. Donne, Miss Lubow, and me to some convenient place for a chat. When we are finished, Miss Lubow will take that person back to his or her place on the tour and return with someone else. When the tour here is complete, we shall go on to the next site and pick up where we have left off. When we have finished, no one will have missed more than fifteen or twenty minutes of any tour, and I will have had all my questions answered. Fifteen or twenty minutes is nothing. If you've seen one winery, you've seen them all."

He scanned the room, as if ferreting out any more doubters. "Then, once I have defined the identity of the perpetrator, I will make an announcement. If, when I have questioned you all, I do not have sufficient information, I will dismiss you and move on to other sources. But I guarantee that, by the end of our little gathering, I will have unmasked the criminal. Now, who will be first?"

An elderly man in a tan Palm Beach suit raised his hand. "It would be a privilege to be first, Mr. Poole." The man spoke with a southern accent.

"Splendid," Poole replied. "Mr. Benedict has provided an example for all of you. Mr. Goodyear?"

Our host, who had been standing nearby looking bemused this whole time, came forward. "May I start the tour, Mr. Poole?"

"Indeed. But only after conducting me to a suitable area for questions. Everyone, please be ready at a moment's notice."

JIM GOODYEAR SHOWED us to a room that boasted a small conference table. Poole indicated the room's suitability, and the rest of the crowd shuffled off with Jim in the lead and the Taylors at the rear.

The four of us seated ourselves in plush leather chairs that surrounded the table. "Let us begin," Poole said. "Miss Lubow, you will please take notes?" She pulled out a pad and pen and sat poised, awaiting the first piercing question.

Arthur Benedict owned a well-known restaurant in Charleston, South Carolina. I knew this because my father possessed one of several cookbooks he'd published. Maybe Dad could prepare something from it that evening, I thought. Maybe old Arthur could come over too, and they could double-team Poole.

The fat man fixed our subject with a steely stare. "Mr. Benedict, are you trying to kill me?"

Nothing like the direct approach. Benedict smiled, a nice old-man smile that reached from his mouth past his eyes and right to his hairline. "Of course not, Mr. Poole. Although I might have some justification."

"I have no idea what you're talking about."

"Your review. Three and a half years ago. You said some terribly mean things about Benedict's. Our crab cakes were mealy and our pork chops mushy. And you totally trashed, as the young people say, our dessert menu. You compared it to street carts in Tijuana."

"And for this you desire to kill me?"

"Not at all. But there might be someone who would. There're some real loonies in this business." Benedict took a hard look at Poole, and the realization dawned. "You really don't remember, do you?"

"Well, I—"

"You don't, I can see it in your face. How funny. How absolutely funny."

"Mr. Benedict, I—"

"Here's the odd thing, though. You were right. We were doing an awful job with our pork chops right around then. Just couldn't get the right pigs, I guess. But our crab cakes—you had no right to say anything bad about those. They've always been the best in the Carolinas."

"What about the desserts?" I asked, trying to be helpful.

"We were having a bad time with the custards that evening, because our oven was on the fritz. But everything else was A-1. But you know what, Mr. Poole? None of that mattered. Because whatever you do, you're good for the restaurant business. You attract a lot of attention, you get people interested in eating well, and in the long run you bring folks in. So if you're a bit of a grouch sometimes, who cares?"

Poole's lips moved, but all that came out were little popping noises as tiny bursts of air exited. Finally he squeezed out, "A bit of a grouch?"

"I meant that in the best possible way," Benedict said. "Now, if you'll excuse me, I'd like not to miss any more of the tour."

He stood up and cocked his head at Carla. She cocked hers at Poole, and he gave a little wave of dismissal. She escorted Benedict out of the room. Just before she exited I noticed a little smile on her face. She may have been protective of Poole, but that didn't mean she couldn't be amused by his silliest behavior.

I gave him a few seconds to simmer, or whatever cooking term you'd like to apply, then said, "Not quite the auspicious debut as a detective you'd hoped for, was it?"

He gave me a regal glare. "On the contrary. I got exactly what I wanted out of him."

"Which was?"

"All will be revealed presently."

I shrugged. If he wanted to waste my time for nine hundred dollars a day, it was okay by me.

We sat for five, ten, fifteen minutes. We stared at each other. We made small talk. I got up and checked out the entry hall. The counterwoman waved. I waved back.

Finally I heard clicking footsteps, and Carla returned, with another NAMESie in tow—some gangly bird wearing shorts, sandals, and a wispy beard. He was complaining about missing the barreling room, and Carla told him that he could see the barreling room at the next place.

"You've seen one barreling room, you've seen them all," I said as they walked in. Then, to Carla: "What took you so long?"

"We couldn't find them."

"This isn't that big a place."

"They'd detoured. They were up over one of the hills."

"Some of them may be over the hill, I agree, but—"

She gave me a chilly look that shut me up. I escorted them to their seats. Poole asked a bunch more dopey questions. The bearded guy answered, managing to work in several fawning remarks. The interview ended ten minutes later, with no one knowing any more than they had before. Unless, of course, some utterly unfathomable process was going on inside Augustus Poole's brain.

By the time we'd gotten through a half-dozen interviews, I was nodding off. The group had returned and made its way to the tasting room off the entry hall. Poole insisted on carrying on with his process while they sipped. Fortunately we found one NAMESie who was in alcohol rehab, and he agreed to skip the tasting.

Then we were done at Goodyear. Poole wanted to cut another from the pack and interrogate him on the way to the next winery, but I managed to talk him out of it. I told him that the interrogee would likely be uncomfortable in a moving car, and we might miss some important clue. Poole reluctantly agreed.

Our next destination was Boot Canyon Vineyards, which is one of the bigger, more commercial places around. Except for Ozzie Cole, they produce more wine than about anyone in the valley, but they manage to keep their quality at a reasonable level. They use some of the profits from their bigger sellers to support a small line of higher-quality wines, under the label Canyon Célèbre. I happened to know Poole had raved about their latest

pinot noir release in his newsletter a month or two back. I
wondered if he'd even remember.

It turned out the memory problem wasn't quite as bad as
that. As soon as we got there, he demanded a bottle. He didn't
like the room that Gary Simpson, Boot Canyon's owner, offered
as an interview space, insisting the tasting room had a better
ambience. So there we sat, amid the displays, and went on with
our tedious process. It was more of the same, except Carla took
care this time to find out the group's route, and Gary had a map
of the place that he'd marked up.

By then I'd also managed to get everyone to introduce themselves to me. My lady friend from Miami turned out to be Stella
O'Neill. It also turned out the guy from New York at our dinner
table last night was her ex-husband, Victor. They were still business partners in two related French restaurants, each called Chez
O'Neill, in their respective cities.

Stella's questioning went like this:

AUGUSTUS POOLE: Why do you want to kill me?
STELLA O'NEILL: That's the silliest thing I ever heard.
AP: Have I ever said anything bad about your estab-
     lishment?
SO: Don't you remember? Five years ago, you said we
     were overrated. You compared our lobster bisque to
     Campbell's Soup.
AP: Did you see any suspicious activity last night, anything
     that didn't seem right to you, anyone acting strangely?
SO: No.
AP: Are you sure? No unfamiliar faces, no lurking figures.
     No one with an unexplained bulge that might have
     been a bottle of poison?
SO: I already told Lieutenant Fitch. I'd like to help you,

but like everyone else I left right after the banquet. I was in bed shortly after that. As I understand it, nothing horrible happened until much later.

AP: Very well, then, thank you for your help. Miss Lubow, please bring Mrs. O'Neill back to the tour and retrieve our next witness.

While Poole was interrogating these poor people, I was observing their reactions. There wasn't one twitch, one facial expression, nothing that expressed any emotion other than exasperation—when they weren't falling all over themselves to suck up to Poole.

Then we came to Monique Forsythe, and things finally got interesting.

She was to be our last interview at Boot Canyon. The NAMESies were in the corridor outside the tasting room, indulging in assorted alcoholic treats, as well as a nice spread of cheese, crackers, and fruit. The Forsythe woman entered, and unlike the others, she wasn't going to take any of Poole's guff. She sat down across the table from him. I stood next to a wall that was all glass.

Carla stood beside me. "I don't trust this one," she whispered.

"Why not?"

"She clearly has a chip on her shoulder about Mr. Poole."

"Does that mean she isn't ready to fawn over him at the slightest provocation?"

Carla frowned. "She worries me, that's all."

Poole made his standard opening. "Ms. Forsythe, are you trying to kill me?"

Monique Forsythe smiled. It was a lovely smile, one that you thought might have been more ready when she was younger. Now it had been touched by a couple of decades of hard knocks.

"Gus Poole," she said. "Has it really come to this?"

Carla drew in an audible breath. Poole sat up straighter and pushed back into his seat. He did that thing where he brought in some air and let it out in quiet puffs. Only this time he forgot to let it out, and he sat there looking like a chipmunk.

He finally let out his lungful of air. "I'm sure I don't know what you are referring to."

"Please stop playing games." She glanced over her shoulder at Carla and me, then turned back to him. "Is it these other people in the room? Would you feel more comfortable if they left?" Back to us. "I think it best if you two left Gus and me alone. Would you mind joining the others outside?"

"I'm supposed to be Mr. Poole's bodyguard, ma'am," I said. "It's my responsibility to stay with him at all times."

Ms. Forsythe smiled again. She leaned across the table to address Poole more intimately. "You don't really think you need to be guarded from *me*, do you?" He didn't reply. She sat back. "I thought not. Please, Mr. Donne, leave us for a few moments."

"I need to hear it from him," I said.

"It's all right, Mr. Donne," Poole said. "You may wait outside. You too, Miss Lubow. Everything will be fine."

I shrugged. "You're the boss."

I took a step to the door, realized Carla hadn't followed, and went back for her. I tugged on her elbow. "Come on. You heard him. They'll be fine."

I managed to usher her out of the tasting room and shut the door behind us. The NAMES members outside were like a hungry army of ants. It was about three-thirty by then, and I gathered some of them hadn't gotten around to having lunch. The empty-stomach theory was supported by my observation as we left

Goodyear that some of the members seemed more affected by one or two glasses of wine than they should have been.

Then, without warning, the door to the tasting room flew open. Out strode Monique Forsythe, wearing an expression of intense anger. She slammed the door shut behind her, took three, four, five steps into the lobby. She stopped, only then seeming to notice the assembled throng.

Something new joined the anger on her face. I couldn't put my finger on it; maybe it was pity, maybe amused tolerance. Whatever it was, it made the woman burst into mocking laughter, a nasty sound that hurt to hear it.

"You'll find him in there," she said.

Something about the way she said "find" galvanized me. I took two running steps toward the tasting room, then realized that Ms. Forsythe was moving toward the exit.

"Stop her!" I shouted.

The woman was already at the door, and still no one had made a move. I was about to rush over and grab her myself, when Carla pounced like a hungry lioness. She forced the older woman to the floor, twisting her hands behind her back and sitting on her.

Ms. Forsythe hissed, "Get *off* me!"

Carla pulled the woman's hands tighter behind her. "Not on your life."

Some other people finally joined Carla in holding the woman down. As soon as I decided she was under control, I dashed to the door and into the tasting room—where I found Augustus Poole.

He stood by the window, hands behind his back, his fingers knitted together. He was staring out at the greenery, oblivious to the commotion that had been going on outside the door. He didn't look at all like the imperious character I'd spent the last two days in the company of. He looked like a sad middle-aged man. He also wasn't dead. Not even close.

I stood in the doorway and waited a few seconds for him to notice me. When he didn't, I said, "Are you all right, Mr. Poole?"

"Hmm?" he said. It took a moment for him to figure out who I was. When he did, he said, "Ah, Mr. Donne. At my side, as usual."

"I thought maybe Ms. Forsythe'd killed you."

Just like that, the old Poole was back. "And if she had, it would have been your fault. Some bodyguard you are. Leaving me alone in my time of greatest peril."

"You ordered me to go," I said. "I specifically offered to stay, and you told me to go outside."

"If I tell you that again, you will please disobey me. It is apparent that I am in more danger than I suspected."

"In what way?"

No response. He turned back to the window again.

Certain that he was okay, and that Monique Forsythe wasn't a threat, I decided it would be a good idea to let her go. I walked out, pushed my way back through a crowd of gawkers, and sought Carla. She'd relinquished her position atop Ms. Forsythe and stood in the middle of the room, scared and brave at the same time.

"Is he—?"

"All right?" I nodded. "Mr. Poole is alive and well and ornery as ever." I moved over to where several NAMESies had Monique Forsythe still pressed to the floor. "Let the lady up," I said. "She's guilty of nothing more than having a creepy laugh."

The crew holding down Ms. Forsythe dispersed. One or two of them seemed to be getting a kick out of the experience, including my friend Arthur Benedict, the crab cake king from South Carolina. Finally they were all off her. She rolled over until she was sitting on her haunches. She looked up at me. I held out a hand, but she pointedly ignored it and achieved a standing position all on her own.

"I apologize, Ms. Forsythe," I said. "It seems I've jumped to an unfounded conclusion."

"Oh, shut up," she said. "I'm lucky to be alive."

"Isn't that overstating things a little?"

"Maybe I'm entitled to a little overstatement." She checked her clothing and found a little snag on her pants. She scowled. "Not only am I bruised and beaten, but you've ruined my slacks. And all because—"

A sly grin overtook her features. "I'll leave it to Gus to explain."

She brushed herself off some more and opened the door leading outside. "You folks go have your little snack now. I'll be waiting in the van." She stepped out and closed the door behind her.

I considered going after her, but the situation seemed to require my rejoining Poole in the tasting room. By the time I got back there he was surrounded by a covey of cooing epicures. Over and over he repeated that he was perfectly all right. No, he didn't know why Ms. Forsythe might have had such an attitude when she left, and no, she hadn't threatened him in any way, and no, he had no reason to think she might want to kill him.

Finally the fawning was too much even for him, and he took a place behind a table holding some wineglasses. He picked up a bottle of Boot Canyon's pinot, gave the label the once-over, the twice-over, and the unnecessary but dramatically obligatory third-time-over. He produced his own private Screwpull from an inside jacket pocket, opened the bottle—with all necessary flourishes, of course—and poured himself a glass. He held it up to the light from the window, sniffed it, held it up again. He took a taste. Contentment crossed his face.

"Ah," he said. "Very nice for a vineyard of this class."

Another sip. A small sigh. Poole surveyed the crowd and said, "Come, come, everyone. Partake." Sounding very much as if he was responsible for the whole spread. "Please, be my guests."

They needed no further encouragement, and they descended upon the table like a flock of vultures on carrion. Poole managed to be social for half a minute or so, then slipped out of the room.

I accosted him out there. "Mr. Poole, if you're going to be paying me a ridiculous sum of money to bodyguard you, you can't keep me in the dark about things."

"In the dark?"

"Don't play dumb. You were in there with that woman for two seconds, and she came out angry as a hornet and laughing like a banshee. Something worth discussing must have gone on in there."

He gave me a brief appraisal. "Ms. Forsythe is an old acquaintance. We were discussing times past."

I threw up my hands in exasperation. "Fine. If she comes back later and bumps you off, don't blame me."

I stormed away toward the front door with the intention of tracking down Ms. Forsythe and getting it out of her. But I spotted Carla and stopped. She'd pulled the curtains away from a window and was peeking out.

"What are you looking at?" I asked.

"That Forsythe woman. I've been watching her since she went outside. She smoked a cigarette and threw the butt to the ground. She made no effort to pick it up."

"See?" I said. "I knew she was a criminal."

"This isn't funny," Carla said. She came away from the window and straightened the curtains. "You watch her for a while. I have to tend to Mr. Poole."

Away she went to do just that. I assigned myself to window duty for a time. While I watched, Ms. Forsythe smoked another cigarette. She threw the butt on the ground. Then she picked it up, and something else too. Maybe the other butt, I decided. She was changing her evil ways already.

I gave up watching Monique Forsythe when she lit her third cigarette. My stomach was rumbling. I returned to the tasting room, where everything was gone except a few bits of cheese that clung bravely to the red wax they use to wrap it with, and an inch of pinot noir in one last bottle. Gary could have brought out more wine, but he looked ready to get that crowd of scavengers out of his place.

I picked up the bottle of pinot, but couldn't find a clean glass. I took a look around, figured what the hell, and drank it straight from the bottle. Poole was right, I thought. Not bad.

Poole was standing by himself at the window again, giving off vibes that he wanted to be left alone. That didn't include me, I decided.

"Mr. Poole?"

He turned to me. "Yes?"

"I think they're about ready to move on to the next winery. Maybe we should get a jump on them and get set up over there first. There's still a few people you haven't spoken to."

"I'm not going," he said.

He was troubled, but whether it was fear or something else I couldn't tell. "You mean you're giving up detecting?" I asked.

"That's exactly what I mean. I was a fool to get involved in the first place. Far too many skeletons to be uncovered."

"Skeletons involving Ms. Forsythe?"

"Among others."

"What's that supposed to mean?"

"It's none of your business," he said.

"It's my business if it's going to affect my ability to keep you out of harm's way."

"It will not." He heaved a sigh. "I'm tired. May I suggest we return to your home? I'd like to take a nap before dinner."

"Whatever you say. I'll play host, and you'll play guest. My father will make us a nice dinner, then we'll all sit around and play Scrabble. Maybe by tonight Lieutenant Fitch will have figured this whole mess out, and we can spend our day tomorrow doing other nice things."

"That would be—nice." He smiled at me, and I smiled back, and before I knew it, wonder of wonders, I was sharing a chuckle with Augustus Poole.

WE GOT HOME a little after four. Poole went directly to his room. Carla said she was tired too, so I suggested she try the big plush couch in the living room. I went to the bathroom. When I came out I checked on Carla; she was watching a local news station from L.A. Something about a new twist to the old high-speed freeway chase story. She looked up, threw me a weary wave, and returned her attention to the TV.

I went into the kitchen, checked the fridge, and came out with a bottle of Amstel Light and some leftover fried chicken. When it was left over from I wasn't sure, but I was reasonably certain it had been since the previous weekend. There was a drumstick, a thigh, and two wings.

As I gnawed on one of the wings, I thought about the night before. Poole had been in the kitchen at Rancho Calzada. I pictured him there, in his yellow pajamas, stuffing chicken wings much as I was now. Meanwhile, Nicky Paoletti was sneaking into Poole's bungalow, stealing the bottle of Chateau d'Yquem, and preparing to drink his death.

Something was wrong with that picture.

What it was I couldn't figure out yet, but it had something to do with the wine. When exactly would somebody have poisoned it? How did they know Poole wouldn't open it right there at the reception, offer to share, and in the process knock off several more members of NAMES? Maybe the killer didn't care. In fact, maybe he or she *wanted* that to happen, so that there would be more openings in the organization, so they could get in if they weren't already, or get some of their friends in if they were.

Or maybe it was suicide. Nicky Paoletti stole the wine, dumped some cyanide in, and drank it. Because he wanted to go out enjoying what was possibly the best dessert wine in the world.

After thinking all that over, I decided it would be a good idea to check in with Brad Fitch. At the least he could tell me where Monique Forsythe was staying.

But first there was another telephone event to take care of— Maggie McKenney. Whose turn had it been to call? I wasn't sure.

I went into my office and checked my machine. Two calls. The first was someone trying to sell us an attic ventilation kit. The second was Maggie. "Hi, Jack," said her voice on the tape. "Looks like I missed you again. I'm just here in the office for a little while—it's around three—and then I have to go off to see another client. I'll call again later. Bye."

Suddenly I had the feeling I wasn't alone. I looked up and there was Carla in the doorway. She'd helped herself to a beer, and held the bottle in her hand.

She smiled. "I get tired of wine sometimes." She pointed her bottle at the phone. "Girlfriend?"

I nodded. "We go in spurts. Sometimes I don't see her for weeks at a time, because of our schedules. Speaking of which, I guess yours doesn't leave you much chance for a social life. What with the traveling and all."

"I don't go out much," she said. "I'm kind of married to my job. God, that sounds like such a cliché." She held the bottle to her forehead and closed her eyes, enjoying the coolness. "There are a couple of men I see. One in San Francisco, one in Tokyo."

"What about Poole?"

She opened her eyes and gave me a stern boy-are-you-stupid look. I quickly defended myself. "I didn't mean you and him, romantically. You think I'm an idiot? I meant him and anybody. Any women friends?" I thought for a moment. "He's not gay, is he?"

She chuckled. "Even if he were, I wouldn't share that information with you. Just as I wouldn't share information about his women friends, if he had any. You may be a detective, but that doesn't mean I'm going to just tell you all the things I've learned about the man because of my privileged position."

"It could be important," I said. "Maybe some angry ex-lover wants to kill him. Male, female, whatever. Why I'm thinking about this is because of Monique Forsythe. I'm guessing they had a thing in the past."

"Maybe they did," she said. "But—"

"Mr. Donne!"

It was Poole, and it sounded like something was very wrong. I sprang past Carla and flew to his room. She was two steps behind me.

I don't know what we expected to find—maybe him there with a knife in his chest, or some villain with his hands around Poole's throat. But he seemed perfectly all right, standing by the side of the bed, holding a pillow with the tips of his fingers.

"What's the matter?" I asked.

"This pillow," he said, extending it in front of him.

"What about it?"

"It has down in it."

"That's because it's a down pillow."

"I'm allergic to ducks."

"Just the feather part, or the whole duck?"

"The whole thing. I can't eat duck meat. I swell up like a blimp."

I refrained from the obvious. "Maybe it's goose down."

"I can't afford to take that chance. Please, may I have a foam pillow?"

"Let me see if there's one in the house."

I went down the hall to the linen closet and dug out an old foam pillow, threw a case on it, and brought it back to the guest room. I placed it on the head of the bed and took the down one from him. "There," I said. "Now you can just take a nice nappie-nap." I left the room, then stuck my head back in. "Is there anything else you're allergic to I should know about?"

"Just ducks."

"All right, then. Dinner will be at seven-thirty. See you later."

Carla and I were halfway down the hall when he called, "Mr. Donne!"

I returned. "What now?"

"The tissue."

"What tissue?"

"The toilet tissue."

"Oh," I said. "That tissue."

He'd knocked the roll under the bed while lifting up the down pillow. I got on my hands and knees to retrieve it, tossed it on his bed, and escaped. At last.

I FOUND MY father in his room, poring through a stack of cookbooks. He looked up when he heard me come in. "Hi, son. There's a message for you from Maggie on the machine."

"I heard it."

He indicated the cookbooks. "I'm trying to figure out what to make for dinner. I'm feeling the need to do something special."

"Why?"

"How often do I have a world-famous food critic in the house?"

"He's already disposed to enjoy your cooking. He'd probably love it if you just made hamburgers."

Dad grinned. "I *was* thinking about steak tartare."

"Raw meat?" I said. "Spare me."

OF THE TWO calls I'd planned to make, the one to Maggie had been preempted. I had to talk to Fitch first.

I began to dial his number at the sheriff's department sub-station in Santa Ynez, then changed my mind and dug out his beeper number instead. It had been moldering in the recesses of my wallet since the Ozzie Cole affair.

My phone rang barely a minute after I'd beeped him. I picked it up. "Brad?"

"Jack? How come you didn't just call me at the office? That's where I am."

"I thought if your superiors were there they might be impressed that people were actually paging you."

"What can I do for you?"

"What's happening with the Paoletti investigation?"

"I thought you were staying out of it."

"I am, as far as taking an active part. But I thought if you'd identified any likely suspects I ought to know about them. Since I'm Poole's bodyguard, and since it's him they're really after. You've figured that out by now, haven't you?"

"I guess so," Fitch said. "Though we're still looking at it from a couple of different points of view." A pause. "Okay, here's the scoop. I talked to all the NAMES people this morning. Nobody saw anything, nobody knows anything. Makes sense, since they all left way before the murder went down. But one thing I did figure out from talking to them."

"That any number of them had a reason to hate Poole?"

"Yeah," Fitch said. "How'd you know?"

"First of all, just from being in the business, I know how many people he's ripped over the years. But it's more than that. Mr. Poole ran his own little interrogation session this afternoon."

"I beg your pardon?"

I told Fitch about the parade of NAMESies through the office at Goodyear and the tasting room at Boot Canyon, about the insipid questioning, and about the lack of any useful information uncovered.

"Why, that fat son of a bitch," Fitch said. "I ought to throw him in jail for interfering with an official investigation."

"There was no harm done. Most of them enjoyed the attention. It also made it easy for me to keep an eye on Poole, and it let me gauge everybody's reactions to him. I didn't notice any likely suspects." I paused. "There was one woman who was kind of interesting, though. Monique Forsythe. I got the feeling whatever had gone on between her and Poole was more on a personal than a business level. What was your take on her?"

I heard him shuffling pages. "Monique Forsythe. Age forty-seven. From L.A., where she's lived for the past couple of years. She publishes some kind of trade magazine for people who run restaurants. She used to own two establishments of her own in Boston—one fancy-schmancy, the other more neighborhoody. Neither one was ever written up by Poole."

"That seem odd to you?" I asked. "That Poole never wrote about her when he's had something to say about damn near everybody else in the world?"

"It didn't at the time I was talking to her, but now you're making me think maybe it should."

"What was your impression of her?"

A few seconds of silence. "She actually seemed like one of the more levelheaded of that bunch. One of the few you could imagine sitting down to dinner with and not thinking they're a pain in the ass by dessert."

Fitch's tolerance for foodies was obviously as low as my own. "Not that I think she'd be behind anything," I said, "but could you check into her some more? Maybe it'll tell us something about Poole. Remember his notion that whoever's after him is 'someone from his past'?"

"I suppose I can give somebody in Boston a call. Probably not until tomorrow, though. It's well into the night shift there."

"Thanks. You get a report back from the lab yet?"

"Just as we thought. The dregs in the glass had enough potassium cyanide in them to kill a man in a few minutes."

"Even somebody as big as Poole?"

"Even him. So much that the lab said they were surprised Paoletti didn't taste something wrong right off. Though even if he did, he'd probably already taken in enough to kill him."

"Anything else?"

"The prints on the bottle included Paoletti's and Poole's, and some others we haven't—"

"Hold on. Poole had his fingerprints on file someplace?"

"Get this. He was in the marines, back in the sixties. He served in Vietnam. Can you imagine?"

I tried to picture Augustus Poole traipsing through the jungle, dressed in camouflage fatigues and carrying an M-14. He must have been a lot skinnier then. But even so, it was a crazy image. "Not hardly," I said. "Who else's prints?"

"Nobody that shouldn't have handled the bottle."

"What about the glass?"

"Just the victim's."

Which supported Poole's recollection that he'd picked up only the bottle. Good. "What did you find out about Paoletti?"

"Gee, Jack, I thought you just wanted to know this stuff so you could protect your client. I don't see how knowing about Paoletti can help you with that."

"Just give with the short version, okay?"

"Then I've got to get off the phone. "Paoletti was a real rising star in the cooking world."

"This I know," I said. "Tell me about *him*, not his reputation."

"He came from back east—"

"Boston?" I asked hopefully.

"Give it a rest, okay? Born in Italy, emigrated to New Jersey when he was a kid. I found he was with the CIA, and I got all excited. Then I found out—"

"That the CIA is the Culinary Institute of America. Who told you this?"

"Roger Platt, who runs the restaurant in Montecito where Paoletti works. *Worked*, I should say. Platt came up in the morning as soon as he heard. Jesus, is *he* crazy. Not only did he lose his chef, but it sounded like they were pretty close too."

"Close? You mean—?"

"Exactly. But also a close working relationship. Their romantic relationship apparently broke up a few months ago."

I said, "So Paoletti went to the CIA, and—?"

"He came out to California six years ago. Been working for Platt for four years as the main man. Nothing much interesting beyond that." Another pause. "I got to get off the phone."

"Just a few more questions—"

"Jack?"

"Yeah?"

"Leave the police work to the police, okay?"

"Whatever you say, Papa."

"Just see that you do."

The next time Poole hollered, I was able to determine that it wasn't a cry of alarm. I found him lying in bed with the top sheet mounded over his enormous form. Only his head poked out.

"I'm hot," he complained.

"The air-conditioning is on."

"It's not helping."

"Take off your sheet and ventilate yourself."

"I had the sheet off. I only covered myself for propriety's sake when I called you. I was hot without it too."

"I don't know what else I can do."

"Isn't there another room that's cooler?"

I hesitated a beat too long. "Not really."

"Not *really?*"

"Not at all."

"You said 'not really.' As if there might be some room for discussion."

"There isn't."

"I'm growing impatient, Mr. Donne."

I sighed. "My bedroom tends to stay a little cooler than this one."

"Then I shall move there."

"*This* is the guest room."

"While I am here, your room will be the guest room."

Sometimes you just know when it's hopeless. This was one of those times. "All right. I'll shift you over to my room."

"You'll see to it that I have all fresh linens, of course."

"Of course."

"And turn the mattress too, please. Both ways. Over *and* end to end."

"Your wish is my command."

He scowled. "I believe I've already pointed out that your humor is starting to wear thin on me."

I sighed again. "It's wearing a little thin on me too."

I WENT TO my room and changed the sheets and pillowcases. I didn't do anything to the mattress. How was he going to know? I took whatever personal items seemed like a good idea to take and brought them back to the guest room. I dumped my load, then escorted Poole to his new quarters. He had on his yellow robe over his undershorts and T-shirt. When we got to my room he asked, "The mattress has been turned and rotated?"

I told him it had. I don't think he believed me, but he didn't press the matter. I left him there and went back to the guest room, where I stripped that bed, threw the bedclothes in the hamper, and put on a new set. He'd only been in the bed a little while, but I didn't wish to rub my skin against material that had been rubbing against his.

I wondered where Carla might be, so I tracked her down. She was in the living room, curled up on the couch, asleep. On the TV was an entertainment reporter from Channel 5 in L.A., blathering on about some action-adventure star. The actor was apparently an inspiration to young people everywhere. I happened to know that the star in question had been arrested a few times for drug offenses and battering his wife. Some inspiration.

In the kitchen my father was preparing four tenderloins of beef. A plate of freshly washed potatoes stood by the sink. Dad was cutting up vegetables—peppers, tomatoes, mushrooms, zucchini we'd grown ourselves—and skewering them. I asked if I could help, but he said everything was under control. He reminded me that I'd had a poor night's sleep and maybe I should take a nap too. He was just trying to show his concern, in his fatherly way.

I was afraid if I lay down I wouldn't wake up till tomorrow morning, so instead I went outside for a walk among the vines. Our grapes were ripening nicely. If the weather held, we were going to have a good year.

I plucked a caterpillar off one of the stalks. It was an odd little bug, green with reddish-brown hairs and two eyelike spots near what I guessed was the rear end. I dropped it on the ground and raised my foot to squash it. Then I stopped, picked it up, and carried it out to the brush beyond the vineyard, where I laid it carefully on a small bush. Getting soft in my old age.

On my way back to the house, I found myself counting the hours until I would be rid of Poole. It was difficult, because I didn't know exactly when we'd be heading back to Bakersfield and beyond on Sunday. Then I thought about what I might do with the money he was paying me. Maybe Maggie and I could take a little trip—that is, if I could ever manage to get hold of her in order to plan it. In the meantime, there was nothing else to do but get ready for dinner.

. . .

"MR. DONNE," POOLE was saying to Dad, "this was a fine steak, superbly grilled. A splendid meal. Absolutely splendid."

It was around eight-thirty. The sun had set, and as soon as it had the temperature seemed to drop by fifteen degrees. Looking out the kitchen window, I could see the last of the light filtering from the western sky.

"It was nothing, Mr. Poole," my father said.

"Nonsense. Wherever did you pick up such well-marbled beef? Is it Argentinian? Kobe?"

"It's from Ralph's." Seeing the look of incomprehension on Poole's face, Dad explained, "A local supermarket chain. They're all over the place."

"What a find, what a find. It was positively succulent. And these skewered vegetables—whatever did you marinate them in?"

"A little vinegar and oil, some spices. Nothing fancy."

"Mr. Donne, you really are quite a cook," Carla said.

"Please, dear. Call me Ray."

"It's true, Ray. Mr. Poole—" She paused. "If I may speak for you, Mr. Poole?"

He bowed.

Carla went on. "Although he's very much a proponent of American home-style cooking, he rarely finds any he truly enjoys. Is that a fair statement, Mr. Poole?"

"I couldn't have put it better," said Poole.

"I'm flattered," Dad said.

"You really should consider putting your cooking before a wider audience," Carla said. "You could open a small restaurant right here at the winery. Just host a few people a night, make it very select but very casual at the same time. Serve a prix fixe menu to keep things simple. I think you'd also boost your wine sales."

"Indeed," agreed Poole.

"I'll consider it," Dad said. Which scared me a little, since he almost sounded like he meant it.

"See that you do," said Poole. "And now, what have we for dessert?"

"I'm afraid I haven't prepared anything," Dad said.

"No dessert?" Poole's lip quivered. He looked like a disappointed five-year-old.

"How about we go out for ice cream?" I suggested.

"A *wonderful* idea!" Poole beamed. "Ice cream, the all-American dessert, the perfect close to an all-American meal. Yes! Take me for ice cream right now!"

POOLE AND I clambered into Uncle Gerry's Seville, leaving Dad and Carla behind to clean up the dishes. We drove into San Tomas, to a place called I Scream 4 Ice Cream. Their stock was generally tasty, but the place itself was a dive. Tacky signs advertising various frozen confections lined the walls. Limp counter displays hawked an assortment of candy. The plastic chairs looked like the kind you'd buy in a stack at Kmart, and the tables matched. The lighting was way too bright, with one fluorescent bulb flickering in and out of service. The floors were sticky enough to grab the soles of your shoes.

Poole was appalled. "They actually serve *food* in a place like this?"

The young woman behind the counter wore a buzz haircut and an Alanis Morisette T-shirt. Her nipples showed so prominently through her shirt, she must have just come out of the freezer. She had a wad of chewing gum in her mouth.

"Whatttayawant?" she asked.

"Mr. Poole?" I prompted.

He turned to me with an expression of mortification. "I couldn't possibly eat in a place like this."

"We're getting it to go."

He shook his head. "I cannot believe respectable people patronize this establishment."

"We're here, aren't we? And don't be fooled by bad impressions. What they sell is really very good." I paused. "Look, this is the only place open around here. Do you want some ice cream or not?"

He scanned a list of flavors on the wall and sighed. "Very well." To Crewcut Girl he said, "Let me have—no, no, that's not right. Make it—no, no, not that either." Another sigh. "You choose, Mr. Donne."

"How 'bout Rocky Road?"

"We don't have Rocky Road," said Crewcut Girl, snapping her gum. "We got Nutmallow Surprise. Same thing."

"Okay. We'll have that." I pointed at Poole. "He's paying."

He didn't hear me. He was engrossed in the flavor list. As he studied it he had his shoulders hunched up, as if to prevent the appalling place from reaching out and touching him. Our server scooped out a helping of Nutmallow Surprise into a quart container. A bit of ice cream dribbled on her finger, and she absently licked off the spillage.

Poole saw it, shrieked, and ran out the door.

I ran after him. By the time I was outside, Poole had climbed into the Cadillac's passenger seat. "Please, take me away from this horrid place," he begged. "Immediately."

Crewcut Girl came rushing out the door. "Hey! Somebody's gotta pay for this!"

"Here," I said, taking out my wallet and tossing her a five-dollar bill. "Keep the change." Sliding behind the wheel, I managed to chirp the tires on the Seville as we fled.

WE WERE ON Highway 154, a mile or so from home, when I saw my Cherokee going by at high speed in the opposite direction. I shouted, "Hey!"

"Is something the matter?" Poole asked. It was the first peep I'd heard from him since we left the ice cream store.

"That was my Jeep."

I looked ahead of me, then behind me, then made an abrupt and dangerous three-point turn in the middle of the highway. Just like that, we were in pursuit.

"Mr. Donne," Poole said nervously. "Would you mind telling me what is going on?"

"Somebody's stealing my car," I said. "I think we should find out who it is."

"Are you sure it's yours?"

"Same model, same year, same dent behind the driver's door. It's dark out, but I'm all but certain it's mine."

Ahead of us, the Cherokee was maintaining a good pace. I had the Seville up to eighty before I started closing. Poole said, "I order you to stop this insane pursuit this instant. We could be killed."

"We're not going to be killed—"

At that moment, whoever was driving the Cherokee must have spied our headlights and realized they were being chased. They sped up. Eighty miles per hour barely kept the distance from widening. I goosed the Seville another five miles an hour. Poole started to protest again until I told him, "Shut up, Mr. Poole." He quieted, clinging for dear life to the dashboard.

Our quarry kept going southeast on 154. Unless I did something soon, I'd be chasing them to Santa Barbara, and the Seville's gas gauge was hovering just above empty.

We were coming up on a sign marking the left turn onto Highway 246 in the direction of the Santa Ynez airport. It also happened to be the turnoff for Rancho Calzada. The Cherokee passed the turnoff for 246 and kept going. I had to catch up soon, or I wasn't going to catch up at all.

I stepped on the gas, and the Seville edged up to ninety. Ninety-five. A hundred. What few cars were going in the opposite direction went by like special effects in a science fiction movie.

We were gaining.

The thing about vehicles like my Cherokee is, unless you're used to driving them, they can get scary past a certain point. Evidently that point was eighty-five for that particular driver and my particular Cherokee, because soon we were close enough for me to read the license plate. It was my car, all right.

I was also close enough to determine the outline of whoever was driving the Cherokee in my headlights. I considered what to do. Bump them from the back? Bad idea—that could mess up both my car and Uncle Gerry's.

I never got the chance to decide on a course of action, because the Cherokee suddenly veered left, then lurched to the right and slid off onto the shoulder, spewing up gravel. Out of control, it wobbled into a ditch paralleling the highway, its speed dropping as the driver struggled to avoid running head-on into the trees lining the road. The car shuddered and ground to a halt. I could see its right front tire on the driver's side bent at an awkward angle, down and inward.

I pulled off the road, braked to a stop, and told Poole to get his head down. Whoever was in the Cherokee might be carrying a gun—which made me wish I'd brought along the 9-millimeter Browning automatic I keep at home. While I was still debating whether to go ahead and sneak up on the Cherokee anyway, the driver's door opened.

Carla Lubow got out—shaken, scared, and speechless.

SHE WAS SAYING, "I'm sorry, but I didn't know it was you."

She was in the Seville's backseat, sitting behind Poole. In the dim illumination provided by the interior light, I watched her face in the rearview mirror. I'd made her get in the Seville; no sense standing by the side of the road and getting run over by some birdbrain.

She might have been telling the truth—she was too frightened for me to be sure. "It makes sense to me," Poole said, and I threw him a stern look: You keep out of this.

Carla spoke up. "What would you have done? There I was driving along, and all of a sudden somebody's on my tail. When I sped up, they sped up. I thought it might be someone trying to kill me." She took a deep breath, held it, let it out. "You can't fault me for trying to escape."

"No," I said, turning around to face her. "But what were you doing in my car in the first place?"

"I was trying to save you some trouble. I just thought, why should you have to come home just to go out again and take me back to Rancho Calzada, and then drive all the way home again? I told your father what I was thinking, and he said it would be all right for me to use your Jeep and bring it back tomorrow. He didn't think you'd mind."

"But you drove right past the turnoff for Rancho Calzada."

"Did I? I didn't even see it. I don't know these roads very well. Besides, I was scared half out of my mind."

"You see?" said Poole. "A perfectly reasonable explanation. Now can we all just go home and get to bed?"

"Not until we get in touch with Triple A," I said. "We can't just leave my car in a ditch, and obviously it's in no condition to be driven."

"Can't it wait until morning?" asked Poole.

"No."

I called the auto club on Uncle Gerry's car phone. Then I phoned Dad so he wouldn't worry. For a moment I even considered chastising him about letting Carla take my car. But what would be the point?

WHEN THE TOW truck arrived, we discovered that the Cherokee had a broken front axle. The truck driver was from the garage in Santa Ynez where I had the car regularly serviced, so it was no problem getting him to agree to haul it there and leave it overnight, as long as I promised to show up first thing in the morning to settle up accounts.

I drove Poole and Carla to Rancho Calzada, where she picked up a change of clothes and an overnight case. Given her unsettled emotional state, Poole had decreed that instead of sleeping in her bungalow, she too would spend the night at my house. The guest bedroom vacated by Poole earlier that day would be hers. Three guesses who would be getting the living room couch.

We finally got home around eleven-thirty. Carla turned in immediately, but Poole wanted a nightcap. After I checked the phone machine and discovered I'd missed yet another of Maggie McKenney's calls, he and I adjourned to the kitchen. I fed him a glass of the amontillado I'd had last night. He surprised me by liking it. "A perfect ending to an imperfect day."

"*Tomorrow* will be a perfect day," I said firmly. "Because we're staying right here. No more gallivanting around playing private eye. We stay home, and we let the sheriff's department do their job. My father can cook some more of his home-style gourmet meals for you."

Poole surprised me again by not putting up a fuss. "That would be acceptable. Just so long as I miss none of my NAMES obligations. After all, my public needs me."

I took in the wide, heavy face across the table and nodded wearily. "I'm glad somebody does, Mr. Poole."

his time the phone was a little more reasonable. It waited until 6:45 A.M. before it woke me up.

I rolled off the couch, stumbled down the hall to the kitchen, and managed to get it on the fourth ring. "Donne Vineyards."

"Jack? It's Brad Fitch. How's everything out your way?"

"I haven't done a bed check yet, but everything seems okay. Why?"

"I'm coming over."

"When?"

"Right now. Make sure Poole's awake when I get there?"

"You want to tell me what this is about?"

"It's a surprise. You like surprises, don't you? This one's a doozy."

"You didn't happen to find out who's been trying to kill Poole, did you?"

"Just wait and see."

The phone clicked in my ear.

. . .

WHEN I KNOCKED on Poole's door there was no response. Since there was an extension phone next to my bed, I figured the ringing had to have awakened him, and he was just playing possum. I knocked a little louder and was met with: "Yes, confound it. Who is it?"

I pushed open the door. There he was, as big as a beached whale, pulling the covers up around his shoulders like a wife caught cheating on her husband. "Mr. Donne," he said irritably, "whatever could compel you to arouse me at this ungodly hour?"

I told him about Fitch's call, and he perked right up. "Splendid," he said. "I will be ready for him in thirty minutes. Have you informed Miss Lubow?"

"I figured at least somebody ought to get some sleep."

A half hour later Dad was also up, making breakfast. I'd managed to work in a shave and shower in his bathroom, and I was just tying my shoes when I heard Fitch's car pulling up outside.

I greeted him at the front door. He took a step in, sniffed, and said, "Ham?"

"Canadian bacon. Dad's making breakfast. Want some?"

"I'd love some. All I've had is some bad coffee and a bran muffin. I hate bran muffins, but I promised my wife I'd try and lay off the doughnuts." He frowned. "Actually I don't have time for breakfast. This is an official visit. Where's Poole?"

"I'll get him. You want to wait for us in the living room? I've turned the couch back into a couch again."

"Huh?"

"Never mind."

Fitch headed for the living room, shaking his head. I went to retrieve Poole from my room. He was dressed, wearing a dark blue suit over a white shirt with faint stripes of a lighter blue.

I led him to the living room, and he took a seat on the couch. Fitch was on his feet. I leaned against a wall. "Mr. Poole," Fitch said as soon as the fat man was seated.

"Yes, Lieutenant?"

"Do you mind going over for me again what you told me yesterday about discovering Paoletti's body?"

"Must I?" He indicated the notebook in Fitch's hand. "I'm sure you have it all in your notes. What's this about, if I may be so bold as to inquire?"

Fitch's expression was guarded. "You say you wandered over to the Taylors' kitchen to nab some chicken wings. Then you came back and went to sleep, but you woke up when you decided your wine was missing. You had"—he leafed through his notebook—"you had 'an odd feeling.' Somehow you knew Paoletti had taken it, so you went over to his bungalow and found him dead. You picked up the bottle to make sure it was yours, then you put it back down on the floor. That's pretty much it, isn't it?"

Poole seemed particularly Buddha-like, sitting with his fingers laced over his stomach. "Is there some reason why we're going over this old ground? If you have something to say, please come out and say it."

"I talked to both Terry Elliott and Ted Taylor last night. Your bottle of wine had been in Mr. Elliott's cellar for several years, and the only person who'd handled it during that time was himself. He gave the bottle to Mr. Taylor, who swears he kept it in his possession until the moment he handed it over to you the other night." Fitch paused. "I just got the lab report on the wine bottle. It turns out that the concentration of hydrocyanic acid in the bottle was considerably less than the concentration in the glass we found on the floor next to Paoletti's body. *Considerably* less."

"I don't get it," I said.

Fitch was eyeing Poole, as if anticipating some reaction. "In other words, there was more poison in the glass than there was in the bottle. Our lab doesn't usually make mistakes with things like this. Their hypothesis is that the killer fed Paoletti a big dose of poison in the glass, mixed with just a little bit of wine, then dumped what cyanide was left into the bottle, just to get rid of it. This make sense to you, Mr. Poole?"

"If you mean does it explain your laboratory's findings," said Poole, "then, yes, it makes sense."

Fitch turned to me. "I knew I should have followed my gut instincts on this, but you got me thinking that it was all about somebody wanting to kill Poole here. Now it looks like Paoletti really was the target all along."

Back to Poole. "And," Fitch said, "that makes you my number-one suspect."

Poole squeezed his eyes shut. He opened them again. Shut again; open again—like he was trying to rid himself of the vision of this pesky policeman. When he concluded it wouldn't work, he said, "And to what feat of legerdemain do we owe this cockamamie conclusion?"

"Come on," Fitch said. "You had a violent argument with the man just a couple of hours before he died. You were the one who found his body. You spent most of the last twenty-four hours playing detective—which would be a swell sort of way to throw suspicion off yourself. If you were me, who would your chief suspect be?"

Poole looked stunned. He swallowed.

"I suppose *I* would," he said at last.

FITCH WASN'T QUITE ready to put Poole under arrest. But he was ready to take the man to the sheriff's department's Solvang substation for questioning.

That's when the trouble began. "You want to take me to a *police* station?" Poole was aghast.

"That's where we generally carry on our interviews with suspects," said Fitch. "Please don't make a scene. If you do, then I will have to arrest you. You wouldn't like that."

"You're just trying to coerce me," snapped Poole. "I'll have none of it. Mr. Donne, please call my attorney."

"I don't know who your attorney is," I said.

"That's fine," Fitch said. "Go 'head and call him. Her. Whatever. Although it may be a while until anybody can make it down here from San Francisco. I'm assuming that's where they'll be coming from? San Francisco?"

"*He.*" Poole's forehead furrowed. "What will happen to me until he arrives?"

"I'll have to keep you at the station."

"That is unacceptable. What if he's not available immediately?"

"I'll have to hold you until he arrives, on suspicion of first-degree murder."

"Hold me? *Hold* me?"

"In a cell. I'll lock the door and put the key where you can't get to it."

Poole sputtered. "But—but—I haven't *done* anything."

"Maybe if you'd answered my questions more satisfactorily, I'd consider letting you go."

They went on like that for a while, until Fitch actually pulled out his handcuffs. At the sight of them Poole leaped up and said, "All right. Take me away. I have nothing to fear because I have nothing to hide."

He turned to me. "Mr. Donne, will you please call Aaron Stevens at Battles, Bracero and Milani in Sausalito. Have him come down here immediately and get me out of this ridiculous predicament."

Back to Fitch. "If I may, I want to be sure my attorney is on his way before I disappear into whatever vile place you intend taking me to."

I went off to my office, called San Francisco information, then called the office of Poole's attorney. I returned a few minutes later. "Mr. Stevens is white-water rafting in Colorado. One of his associates is available, but no one can possibly get down here before Monday morning."

Poole looked stricken.

"We can always find you a public defender," Fitch said.

"A public defender?" Only Poole could have enunciated the phrase one syllable at a time. "That will never do. Why don't we simply postpone this inquisition until Monday?"

"Mr. Poole," Fitch said. "You will come with me *this instant*, or I will place you under arrest."

"Mr. Poole?" I said.

"Yes?"

"My uncle Gerry—my father's brother—is an attorney. He doesn't handle criminal law, but I'm sure he knows someone who does. Would you like me to call him?"

Poole's expression was pained, but he gave in. What was his alternative? "Yes, please, Mr. Donne. I would like that very much."

I CAUGHT GERRY at home. He was aware of Paoletti's murder, since it had been all over the news, but he was flabbergasted to hear that Augustus Poole was under suspicion. When I explained why I was calling, he got me off the phone and called back five minutes later to tell me that his friend Lars Petersen would be waiting for us at the Solvang substation when we got there.

After that I woke up Carla. Explaining the need for the hurry-up, I told her to get dressed ASAP. Then I went and got my gun. After what had happened last night, it seemed wise to start carrying it with me until everything was settled, one way or another.

We skipped breakfast. Fitch allowed me to drive Poole and Carla into Solvang. If Poole ended up getting booked, or if they were there for several hours, I didn't want to be stuck without transportation. Fitch didn't figure Poole was likely to pull anything, and since he wasn't under formal arrest, technically he could go to the station any way he wanted to.

I parked the Seville, and Poole watched me with wide eyes as I placed my gun and holster in the glove compartment. I didn't think it a good idea to have it at the sheriff's station, since it might make some people nervous. Poole said, "Are you sure this Petersen fellow knows what he's doing?"

"I'm not sure of anything," I said. "But if Uncle Gerry recommends him, you can be sure he'll do as good a job for you as anyone."

I didn't want to say that when I heard the name of the man Uncle Gerry had recommended to protect Poole's interests, I'd immediately formed a picture of some blond yokel with a singsong Swedish accent. But I couldn't have been more off. Petersen's suit was as expensive and well-cut as Poole's—Brooks Brothers, I suspected, like my uncle favored. Petersen's eyes were blue and clear, but that portion of his hair that hadn't yet turned gray was black. He was tall, two inches or so taller than me, and just a little overweight. He also had no trace of a Swedish accent.

Poole's temporary lawyer greeted us warmly at the entrance to the Solvang substation. Then he took Poole aside to tell him what to expect.

A little after nine, Poole, Fitch, and Petersen disappeared inside an interview room. Carla made as if to follow, but Fitch told her no way. I stayed out too.

We sat down on a hard bench in the lobby and stared at each other for a while, until I tried to engage her in conversation. She was back to monosyllables. For a while I considered confronting her about her little escapade of the night before. Hey, I would say. I'm pretty sure you're full of shit about last night. Why don't you tell me what you were really up to with my Cherokee?

But I didn't want to make a scene. Plus, I thought, if something really was up, she wouldn't tell me about it anyway.

After an hour, I suddenly remembered Maggie McKenney. Excusing myself, I got up to find a pay phone. I tried Maggie's office, but I got the machine. I tried her home too, just in case. Another machine.

I returned to the bench. Carla wasn't there.

I went over to the desk sergeant on duty, a short Latino guy with a Marine Corps brush cut. "Did you see the woman who I was sitting there with?" I asked, pointing to the bench.

"She went someplace," the sergeant said. "I don't know where."

I fumed, annoyed with myself for letting her slip through my fingers. While Fitch was interrogating Poole, who I still felt hadn't done anything illegal, a truly suspicious character may have escaped.

I was about to go check outside when she returned from the ladies' room. Since I didn't know that's where she'd been, I asked her rather too forcefully where the hell she'd gone. She told me off, in no uncertain terms. We glared angrily at each other for a while, until I blinked first and went back to the bench. After a bit she rejoined me.

"I'm sorry," she apologized. "I guess I'm just on edge. Poor Mr. Poole."

"Yeah," I said. "Everybody's sorry. Including me."

. . .

AROUND TEN-THIRTY, having gotten tired of sitting around and doing nothing, I invited Carla to come with me to the garage where my Cherokee had been towed. The place was only a ten-minute drive away, in Santa Ynez. At first she seemed about to say no, then she shrugged.

She was quiet on the drive over. At the garage, not only was I able to gas up the Seville, but I also confirmed the tow truck driver's diagnosis of a broken front axle. No Jeep for a week to ten days. At least it wasn't a problem getting the tow charges tacked on to my final bill.

Heading back to the substation, Carla kept looking out her window, much the way she had on the way out. I asked her what she was expecting to see.

"Nothing," she said.

At eleven-fifteen I was parking the Cadillac across the street from the substation. Poole and Petersen were waiting outside. Carla spotted them from half a block away, and as soon as I switched off the ignition, she jumped out and ran up to Poole. I trotted along behind her. For a second I thought she was going to throw her arms around him, but she pulled up short, straightened, and simply asked how he was.

"Miss Lubow," Poole said. "I have just been subjected to the most humiliating experience of my life."

I thought perhaps he'd been arrested and booked, and that Petersen had already arranged for his bond. But no, Fitch couldn't come up with anything to make an arrest reasonable.

"So you stuck by your story?" I asked Poole.

"It is *not* a story," he insisted. "It is the absolute truth."

"After a while," Petersen added, "Lieutenant Fitch just ran

out of questions. We convinced him that Mr. Poole's argument with the deceased had been nothing more than a momentary clash between two excitable people. That was that."

"Knowing the lieutenant," I said, "I'm sure he still has his suspicions."

"Oh yes," Petersen said. "But you know, I kind of admire him. He's a real bulldog. He doesn't like to give up."

"Admire him?" Poole grimaced. "The man's not a bulldog, he's a fiend."

AFTER INFORMING US that he didn't think we'd be getting any more trouble from Fitch unless some significant evidence turned up, Petersen made his good-byes. Poole was obviously shaken by the interrogation. As we drove away, I tried to pump him about the session. He wouldn't pump. He seemed lost in thought, sitting quietly in the passenger seat, observing the scenery without interest.

I decided maybe I could get him going if I talked about his favorite subject. "What would you like for lunch, Mr. Poole?"

"I'm sure wherever you take us will be fine."

"What are you in the mood for? Italian? Chinese?"

"You decide. You've done well by me up until now." He paused. "I'm not really very hungry."

Augustus Poole not hungry? Notify the media. I considered taking him home, but Dad had been whipping up quite enough in the way of meals lately, and he could use the rest. And since apparently there hadn't been a poisoning attempt on Poole's life, it seemed okay for us to be out in the open.

"Is it all right if we drive down to Santa Barbara?" I asked. "There's a place I think you might like."

"That will be fine."

"Isn't Santa Barbara rather far?" Carla asked.

"Not really," I said. "And by the time we get there, maybe Mr. Poole will have worked up an appetite."

"Shouldn't we just go back to your place?" she asked.

"I've got a better idea," I said.

❖ 17 ❖

If you didn't know exactly where Roger Platt's Courtyard Café was, there's a good chance you'd never find it. You drive up one tree-lined road, turn off onto another, then again onto a third. There are street signs, but they're often hidden by foliage. Each road is interrupted every so often by a driveway, and up at the top of the ones that don't curve too much you can see houses that scream money, money, money. Finally you come to a dead end. But just before that you make a left and go up one last driveway that cuts through a low stone wall. Voilà.

The place isn't really a courtyard, because it's indoors and has a ceiling. Clinging plants grow up the walls. There are two huge skylights that provide a great deal of light, so you might as well be outside. Except you don't ever have to worry about getting rained on in the winter.

We arrived a little after 1:00 P.M. Nearly every table was filled with diners. I allowed a cute strawberry-blond hostess with a ponytail to seat Poole and Carla while I went off to find Roger Platt.

He was sitting in his tiny office, studying what looked like a balance sheet. I introduced myself—we'd met before, but there was always the possibility he wouldn't remember—and told him how sorry I was about Nicky. Then I asked if he'd like to come out and meet Augustus Poole.

"Oh dear," he said.

"What's the matter?"

"Augustus Poole is here? Now?"

"Is that a problem?"

"Only that the restaurant is not—at its best. What with Nicky gone and all."

"I'm actually a little surprised you're even open."

"We were closed yesterday. I was planning at first to stay closed through the weekend, but my business partners didn't agree. We opened today, and so far things seem more or less normal. But I'm not looking forward to the dinner rush."

"Why don't you come on out and meet Poole?" I suggested. "I'm sure I can convince him that today's probably not the best day to review you. Given what's happened."

He considered for a moment. "All right."

Soon the four of us were seated at a table directly under one of the skylights. I adjusted my chair to get a ficus branch out of my face. A waiter came by, and Platt took the liberty of ordering for us off the menu.

After a few minutes of perfunctory chitchat, I asked him, "So what do you think you'll you do now? About a chef, that is?"

"I imagine I'll find someone. There are always chefs available. They tend to move around a lot. But I'll never find one as good as Nicky."

I sensed something more than a mere business relationship. "You two were close?"

He looked terribly pained, and I didn't feel it was my business to subject Platt to any more emotional trauma than he'd already had, so I moved the conversation on to other things. After a while

I even managed to pull Poole somewhat out of his funk. By the time our meal arrived he and Platt were babbling away about Mongolian grilled goat and Kazakhstani potato pies.

The meal was delicious, but it had the late Nicky Paoletti's imprimatur. Maybe Roger Platt wasn't missing him in the kitchen today, and maybe he wasn't going to miss him tomorrow, but sooner or later, to my thinking, he was going to have to fill a very deep void. I didn't envy him the task.

ON THE WAY back to the valley I took the interior route, along Highway 154. It's a little less civilized—being a two-lane stretch of winding mountain road most of the way—but a lot more scenic. I drove a steady fifty, letting Poole and Carla savor the view. Anyone who wanted to pass me, I'd accommodate by edging over a bit. In a hurry? Be my guest.

We were twenty miles out of Santa Barbara, with another twenty or so miles to go, when I noticed a dark sedan trailing us. The sedan was keeping pace, about a half mile back. At first I didn't mind—if Poole, Carla, and I could enjoy a leisurely Friday-afternoon drive, why couldn't somebody else?

Then the car—a late-model Pontiac—was closer, some two hundred yards behind. As I watched in the rearview mirror, it sped up until it had pulled within a length of the Cadillac's rear bumper. I could see one other person besides the driver, but I couldn't make out if anyone was in the backseat. It didn't look like it, but I couldn't be sure.

Something about the car had my internal alarm jangling. I performed an experiment and sped up to sixty; so did they. I slowed down to forty; they followed suit.

"What are you doing?" Carla asked.

"I think we're being tailed," I said.

She turned around to look. "You mean those two men in that dark car?"

By this time Poole was interested too. He attempted to look over his shoulder at our pursuers, but wasn't able to twist far enough to do so. He grabbed the rearview mirror and yanked it around to take a look.

"Hey!" I yelled, snatching back the mirror and readjusting it. "I'm the driver, I'm the bodyguard, I should be the one to watch the bad guys."

"Bad guys?" Carla said. Fear colored her voice. "You think they're bad guys?"

"It's a relative term. For all we know, it's possible Lieutenant Fitch has just put a tail on Mr. Poole."

"Possible—but unlikely?" asked Poole.

I made a noncommittal grunt. Better if neither of them got frightened, especially since I was starting to feel apprehensive enough for all of us.

No such luck. "You see, Mr. Donne?" said Poole. "Everyone, including you, thinks I'm out of my mind because I insist that someone means to kill me. But I am not out of my mind. The fact that the poison in my wine evidently was meant for Mr. Paoletti does nothing to change that. There are still those other attempts on my life to consider."

"Whoever these guys are behind us, they're not doing anything very threatening at the moment. All they're doing is driving—"

At which point they sped up, zoomed past us, and pulled directly in front. Their brake lights flashed, and I had to jam on my own brakes to keep from rear-ending them.

Moments later, both cars were pulled over to the shoulder of the highway, idling. It was not the kind of behavior a tail from the sheriff's department would be engaging in. Déjà vu all over again, a replay of last night with Carla and my Cherokee—except this time I was the stoppee, not the stopper. I didn't like that.

So as soon as I saw movement inside the Pontiac that indicated someone was getting out, I jammed the Seville into reverse, stomped on the accelerator, shot backward, braked, shifted back into drive, floored it, and peeled off down the road.

I have to hand it to whoever was driving the Pontiac—he had good reflexes. Soon they were back on our tail. If by chance they had guns and decided to start shooting, things were not going to be good. Especially with a target as large as Poole.

After a couple of miles' worth of high-speed pursuit, I decided to chance a tricky maneuver. Coming up to the turnoff for Los Dos Amigos Road, I took it.

It used to be in years past that Cadillacs were big, soft cars for big, soft people. Some still are. But not my uncle's Seville, and not with me at the wheel. The engine complained only a bit as I jammed the car off down Dos Amigos, and the rear end fishtailed only a few degrees. Then we were off, down a stretch of old concrete that I knew turned to gravel after a mile or so.

When I was a kid I used to spend a lot of time down Dos Amigos. A little stream ran through a small canyon that paralleled it, and several ponds had formed. One was a great swimming hole, with a fine rock to jump off and some nice flat ones to sun on. When I was in my early teens, it was a favorite summmertime haunt for my friends and me.

Dos Amigos Road runs mostly straight, so I kept catching glimpses of our pursuers in the rearview mirror. They were doing well for, I assumed, not knowing the road. But Dos Amigos is straight only most of the time, which means that the rest of it is rather curvy. I flung the Seville around one of the curves, and our pursuers were, at least briefly, out of sight.

That I'd headed down Los Dos Amigos Road wasn't due to

any desire to relive my misspent youth. I knew in just a couple more miles it dead-ended in another road, this one dirt. That road was as twisty and turny as it could be, curving around the base of a good-size hill, before it spilled onto a feeder road that would return us to 154. Some of the local juvenile delinquents still held drag races there. One particularly bad spot was our own local version of Dead Man's Curve.

My decision was a snap one, but it was based on two things. First, even though it had been many years since I'd been down this way, I knew where the dirt road led. Second, I'm a damned good driver. I learned how when I was with BATF. Unlike the phony-baloney crooks and law enforcement types who populate most TV shows and action-adventure movies—where everybody knows how to rat-race even the most soft-suspensioned vehicle at a hundred miles an hour through swamp, desert, or jungle—whoever was after us likely wouldn't be able to keep up. No brag, just fact.

It was with no small amount of surprise that I found out I was wrong. They were actually closing.

I made the mistake of muttering a remark to that effect. "Perhaps we should turn and fight," suggested Poole.

I skipped giving him a dirty look in order to keep my eyes on the road. By the time we came to the turn, the Pontiac was less than a hundred yards behind us. We hit the dirt road and kept going.

The trees that had lined Dos Amigos gave way to scraggly brush. Harsh sunlight blasted in through the windshield. Dead Man's Curve loomed ahead—a hairpin to the right. Anyone not negotiating it properly invited a steep tumble down a rocky slope—you come up on it, miss the curve, and all of a sudden you're in midair.

The Seville squealed and squeaked, and we got closer to the

edge of the precipice than I cared to, spraying up rocks and dirt into space. The Pontiac was right behind us, but I knew something its driver didn't. Just when you think you've made it around that right-bearing hairpin, along comes another going off to the left.

I negotiated both curves, barely. There was a feeling of empty air under one of the rear tires for a fraction of a second, but the gods were with us and we managed to avoid any *Thelma and Louise* routine.

The guys in the Pontiac weren't so lucky. They didn't go flying off into space, but the second curve came as a big surprise to them. They lucked out and kept going, but their wheels weren't turned in the right direction. The Pontiac spun around, and fifty yards or so beyond the second hairpin, it toppled over the side of the road. Which wasn't necessarily fatal. Yes, there was a slope where they went down, but it wasn't too steep.

I stopped the Seville.

"What are you doing?" Poole demanded. "Those criminals could climb out of the wreckage, scurry up that hill, and still catch us. All our efforts will be for naught."

"*Our* efforts? All you did was sit there."

"What was I to do, pull out your weapon and shoot at them?"

"Mr. Poole's right," Carla asserted. "We should just drive on into town and get the police. Let them come out here and take care of these people."

"And if these 'people' aren't hurt, what then?" I said. "They're going to walk away, find another car, and come after us again. We have the drop on them now. Let's see if we can't take advantage of that."

I got my gun from the glove compartment, taking it out of its holster. I pushed open the door, got out, and made my way over to the side of the road. I walked back until I could see where the Pontiac lay on its passenger's side, about twenty yards down the slope.

Two arms and a head—a black guy, beefy-looking, his head shaved—were poking out of the driver's window. He was struggling to get out through the window opening, evidently unable to push open the door. From the looks of things he was going to be free soon anyway.

I shouted down, "Hold it right there!"

The fellow escaping from the Pontiac looked around, as if trying to figure out where the voice in the wilderness could be coming from.

"I'm up here!" I shouted.

He stared at me for a few seconds. Then I saw the other guy's hand reach out and drag him back in the car.

"Come on out!" I ordered. "I'm armed! You guys don't have a chance!"

The second guy's head popped up out through the window. I drew a bead on him. "Climb on out of there, both of you! And as soon as you're out, I want you to put your hands up!"

He was looking at me, and I got the opportunity to study his face from a distance. It was a round face with a big walrus mustache, a receding hairline, and tiny ears.

The face broke into a wide grin.

"Jack?" the guy shouted. "Jack Donne, is that really you? You son of a bitch, you wouldn't shoot an old Treasury Department buddy, now, would you?"

t's a trick, hissed a nagging little voice inside my head. How hard would it be for anybody to find out the name of the person guarding Augustus Poole, and use that information in an attempt to ease out of a touchy situation? Not that I understood why anyone might be tailing Poole in the first place.

I kept the man in my sights as I moved closer. "Who are you?" I said.

"Jack, old buddy, I'm hurt you don't remember me." He spoke with a vaguely familiar southern twang.

"Sorry," I said. "But who the fuck *are* you?"

He shook his head, chuckling. "It's Charlie. Charlie Rolfe."

"Charlie—?"

And all at once, everything clicked into place. "Jesus Christ," I said, lowering my gun. "Charlie Rolfe."

"The one and only," he said.

SIXTEEN YEARS AGO, fresh out of the air force, I'd been a trainee with the Bureau of Alcohol, Tobacco and Firearms. I trained at the Criminal Investigative School, Federal Law Enforcement Training Center, in Glynco, Georgia.

Glynco is to special agents of the U.S. Treasury Department what Quantico is to the FBI: Fed school. You take courses in how to maintain surveillance on a suspect, how to participate in raids, how to interview witnesses, how to obtain a search warrant, how to gather physical evidence, how to make a proper arrest, and so forth. Anybody hoping to become a special agent with one of several subdepartments of the U.S. Treasury, including the Secret Service, the IRS, and the Customs Service Special Investigative Division, along with a few others, attends FLETC.

Charlie Rolfe, training at Glynco at the same time I was, was with Customs. We met one Saturday morning on the firing range, the two of us working on our own to get in some extra shooting practice, and became buddies. I hadn't seen him since the year we both graduated and moved on to our respective jobs. But it was Charlie Rolfe, all right. The one and only.

While Charlie and his partner hoisted themselves out of the Pontiac, I looked over at the Cadillac parked twenty or thirty yards away. "It's okay!" I shouted. "Everything's fine!"

A beat. Then Poole's door opened, and he lumbered out. Carla came from the backseat a moment later. They stood beside the car, looking at me with bewildered expressions.

I heard Charlie Rolfe saying, "Can you give us a hand here, Jack?"

He and the other guy—who I assumed was his partner—had reached the top of the slope. Charlie was a good fifteen pounds heavier than when I'd last seen him, and his partner was just as husky and out of shape. I held out a hand to haul first one, then the other, to the roadside.

They were both wheezing. In between breaths, Charlie introduced his partner as Dave Curtis. I gave them a little time to get back their wind, then walked them to the Cadillac. I was saying to Charlie, "I hope you don't mind if we don't catch up on old times just this minute, but what the hell were you doing chasing us?"

We'd reached Poole and Carla. "We weren't chasing you, Jack." Charlie pointed at Carla. "We were chasing her."

"Come again?" I said.

He reached into the pocket of his suit jacket and pulled out a small leather wallet similar to one I used to own. He flipped open the wallet and showed Carla his badge. "U.S. Customs Service," he said, still gasping a little. "I'm Special Agent Rolfe." Indicating his partner: "This is Special Agent Curtis. Are you Carla Lubow?"

She blinked, uncomprehending for an instant. Then awareness lit her eyes. She looked like an animal that had just stepped into a very nasty trap. She nodded before she could catch herself.

"Miss Lubow," Charlie said. "I'm very pleased to meet you. You are under arrest."

I SAID TO Charlie, "You mind starting at the beginning?"

Carla was in the Cadillac's backseat, handcuffed. Dave Curtis was seated beside her, using the car phone to call in to their field office in San Francisco. I'd already used the phone to call the same tow truck guy I'd used yesterday. I was becoming his best customer.

Poole and I were standing outside the Cadillac with Charlie Rolfe, waiting for the tow truck. Charlie said, "The beginning is a fella named Arthur Sakamoto."

"Who's he?"

"A smuggler. One of the slickest working the Pacific Rim. We've been after him for years." He nodded toward the car. "Miss Lubow there is one of his top mules."

Poole frowned. "Mules?"

"Couriers," explained Charlie. "She takes whatever Sakamoto wants carried overseas and delivers it to its final destination."

"Come, come," said Poole, disbelieving. "Miss Lubow has been in my employ for some time. She has been in my presence night and day—within propriety's bounds, of course. Surely if she were engaged in any illegal activity, I would know about it."

"Yeah, well, you're wrong about that, Mr. Poole," Charlie said. "She was carrying on right under your nose. At first we thought you might be in on it too. But we watched you and her long enough to realize you were clean."

Poole was speechless. He just looked confused—and hurt.

"It was very smooth," Charlie continued. "Here she is, working for a man who's enough of a celebrity that he tends not to be bothered by customs pretty much anywhere he goes. Wherever he travels, she travels. Especially to Japan, which happens to be where a lot of Artie Sakamoto's business gets conducted."

"What was she smuggling?" I asked.

"Information, mostly."

I must have had a stupid look on my face, because Charlie chuckled. "Sakamoto is based in San Francisco, but he's most interested in the Silicon Valley. He's more or less exclusively into high-tech industrial secrets—software design, that sort of thing. Easiest stuff in the world to transport, because it's very easy to hide. And Sakamoto's one of the best—or *was*, I should say, till we finally put the bag on him and all his people, two days ago."

He indicated Carla. "All, save one. Imagine my surprise when I went knocking on Mr. Poole's door, and his chef, or whoever the hell he was, tells me they're spending the weekend in the Santa Ynez Valley. With you. It took us till this morning to finally track her down." Charlie chuckled again. "She's lucky we arrested Artie and his other playmates first. They're kind of mad at her."

"What for?" I asked.

"Coming back from her last trip to the Far East, she stiffed 'em out of a hundred K or so in cash. She was just trying to skim a little for herself. Artie found out and tried to scare her into giving his money back. She'd been such a good mule for so long, he didn't want to kill her outright without giving her an opportunity to square things first."

"How'd he do that?" I asked. "Try to scare her, I mean."

"He had one of his goons take a potshot at her in broad daylight, right in the middle of downtown 'Frisco," Charlie said. "Only they missed. On purpose."

Poole found his tongue. "Are you saying that incident was an attempt on Miss *Lubow's* life? Not mine?"

"That's what I'm saying."

Poole seemed to take it as a personal affront. Before he could go on, however, I asked Charlie, "So what happens now?"

"First we wait for somebody to come and haul my car out of that ditch back there. Then you drive Dave and Miss Lubow and me to the nearest law enforcement facility, so I can throw her in the can while I make arrangements to take her back north with us. That okay with you, old buddy?"

"I guess it has to be," I said.

WHILE CHARLIE WATCHED the tow truck drag the Pontiac back up to the road, I called Dad. I told him there'd only be three of us dining tonight—him, Poole, and me. He asked about Carla—who at the moment was sitting behind me in the backseat with Dave Curtis—and I told him that all would be explained when Poole and I got there. Dad then asked me to stop off on the way home and pick up some Mexican beer and corn tortillas. I asked him what we were having to eat that required beer and tortillas, and he told me that two could play at this surprise thing.

A short time later, the five of us were heading for Solvang. Poole and I were in our usual configuration in the front. Carla was sandwiched between the two customs officers in back. Poole wasn't happy about our destination. He didn't want to come within five miles of the scene of his humiliation earlier than morning. But he didn't have a lot of choice.

He was unhappier still when we got to the sheriff's substation and Charlie told him he had to come in to give a statement. "Send someone outside to take it from me," Poole said.

"We don't work that way," Charlie replied.

Eventually we talked Poole into going in. Curtis took Carla away someplace else while Charlie hunted up an interrogation room for Poole and me. We'd been sitting there about twenty minutes when who should walk in but Brad Fitch. I introduced him to Charlie Rolfe.

"So somebody finally caught up with you," he said to Poole.

"Bah," Poole responded. "We are here because Miss Lubow is in trouble. Not I."

"So I heard. What kind of trouble?"

I explained the situation to Fitch. I could tell he hoped that Poole was mixed up in the smuggling ring, but he managed to hold his tongue.

When I'd finished, Fitch said to me, "I've checked out Monique Forsythe. She's clean. No record, no nasty scandals, no nothing."

As I thanked him, one of the deputies came in and told Charlie there was a call from somebody at the customs field office in San Francisco. Fitch left to show Charlie where the phone was.

As soon as we were alone, Poole said, "If I understand this correctly, I will not be able to see Miss Lubow again?"

"Probably not till her case comes up in court," I said. "Unless you want to go see her on visiting day."

He frowned. "I feel like such a fool."

"Why's that?"

"Here she's been in my employ all this time, and it's been nothing more than a front for her criminal activity. Did I use that word correctly? A front?"

"Close enough," I said. "As for feeling like a fool, I doubt you're the first man to be distracted by a nice-looking woman. That doesn't make you not a fool, though."

He snorted, "Bah," and dismissed me with a wave of his hand. I just grinned.

CHARLIE LET POOLE and me go around a quarter to seven. When we got home, Poole summoned Dad from the kitchen to the living room. I let Poole tell the story of our day's adventures, which he recounted with little embellishment. No doubt a consequence of his deeply bruised ego at never having suspected Carla Lubow's deceitfulness.

Finally Poole went off to his—rather, my—room for a brief rest before dinner. After he'd left, I noticed that Dad was looking at me with concern. "Are you all right?" he asked.

"I'm fine."

"This is the second murder case you've gotten mixed up with this year—and the second time you've put yourself in danger on account of it."

"I'm glad you're around to keep score for me."

"One of these days you might get yourself hurt."

I smiled. "I'll finish up with Poole, and as soon as I drop him off on Sunday back at his house, it'll be the end of my detective career." I crossed my heart. "Scout's honor."

He let out a skeptical grunt, took up his quad cane, rose, and creaked off to the kitchen. He paused in the doorway. "By the way, Maggie called. She told me you haven't talked to her in three days. I hope you're not neglecting her."

"Not intentionally," I said.

He grunted again and hobbled off.

I sat on the couch for a time, thinking about what my father had said about me putting myself in danger. In my heart of hearts I knew that I didn't want to be a detective, but somehow these cases just kept finding me. Maybe I should start learning how to say no.

inner turned out to be Dad's green chili stew, the original recipe courtesy of Jesus Fonseca, which made it as close to authentic as you could probably get. To go with the stew we had a nice, simple green salad and the Bohemia beer and fresh tortillas I'd picked up on the way home from Solvang. For dessert we had flan and coffee with Kahlua.

Poole proclaimed that he was yet again impressed with one of Dad's feasts. He eased back in his chair, folding his hands atop his huge belly. "Now that the meal is concluded, I have an announcement to make."

After pausing to make sure he had our undivided attention, he went on. "As you both know, I engaged in some investigative activity yesterday, though I was unable to ferret out the identity of the person who might want to kill me. For the simple reason that, as you also know, there is no such person. This seems clear now. Of those previous 'attempts' on my life, one was actually an attempt on Miss Lubow's." He gave me one of his little bows. "The incident in Napa now seems likely to be merely coincidental, as young Mr. Donne suggested on the train two days ago.

And the poison in my bottle of sauternes seems to have been ingested by its intended victim."

He paused again. "Nevertheless, I believe that I have shown a heretofore unknown aptitude for detective work. Had someone truly been trying to kill me, I feel certain that person would now be behind bars."

Dad and I exchanged looks.

"An injustice," Poole went on, "is being perpetrated. All of us know which injustice I refer to, *n'est-ce pas?*"

"Just so we're on the same wavelength," I said, "why don't you spell it out for all the world to hear."

"The injustice I speak of is that I am under suspicion of murder."

"Oh, that," I said. "Believe me, Lieutenant Fitch will probably get over that. As soon as he catches the real killer."

"Yes, but when will that be? How long must I suffer the slings and arrows of a wrong-minded gendarme? Therefore, I shall take the necessary steps to relieve myself of this burden."

He was cooking now, leading us to his final dramatic revelation: "I shall endeavor to solve this crime myself."

He sat up straighter in his chair, assuming an expression of vast self-importance. He held the expression for a time, waiting for a response. When nobody said anything to reinforce his being so unbelievably wonderful, he turned to Dad. "Well?"

"What can I say?" my father asked.

Poole's attention switched to me. "Well?"

"Like my father said. Only—"

"Only what?"

"Only I thought you were out of your detective phase. I was hoping you were ready to return your full attention to being America's preeminent food and wine critic."

He frowned thoughtfully. "I'll let you in on a little secret,

Mr. Donne. The position you have alluded to—somewhat sardonically, I might add—does not take up a great deal of my time. Far from it. Frankly, of late I have found myself a little bored. I feel I'm ready for new challenges."

He pushed himself away from the table and stood up. "I shall retire to my room, where I can dedicate myself to considering all facets of this baffling case. I may need to use the telephone, so I would appreciate it if you would both refrain from using it. Of course, I will reimburse you for any calls I make. If you send me an itemized bill, I will—"

He caught himself. "Oh, dear."

"What's the matter?" Dad asked.

"I was about to say I would have Miss Lubow send you a check. That will not be possible now, of course." He let out a strained chortle that sounded something like "Hm-hm-hm-hm-hm."

Then he shrugged his massive shoulders. "Another challenge I shall have to face," he said. "Finding a new assistant capable enough to fill Miss Lubow's shoes."

THE DISHES TOOK me half an hour. After that I went into the living room, turned on the TV, surfed through several dozen channels of garbage, and finally settled on a baseball game. The Colorado Rockies were in Los Angeles, up on the Dodgers 6–1. In the ten minutes I watched, the score went to 11–1.

Around the top of the eighth inning, I dozed off on the couch. I had a dream in which Maggie McKenney and Carla Lubow were racing hot rods around Dead Man's Curve, with the winner to have the honor of spending the night with Poole. The loser got me.

I woke up, and there was the man himself, looming over me. "We have an errand, Mr. Donne."

"Where are we going?"

"A bed-and-breakfast establishment called the Ballard Inn. Do you know it?"

I nodded. "What's at the Ballard Inn that can't wait until morning?"

"Monique Forsythe," Poole said.

FORTY MINUTES LATER we were parking in front of the Ballard Inn, Ballard being a hamlet about halfway between the towns of Santa Ynez and Los Olivos. Though the inn was only a dozen or so years old, it was designed to look older—a two-story, fifteen-room, neo-Victorian clapboard structure with white gingerbread trim and a broad front porch complete with wicker rocking chairs.

The first floor was inviting, all wood paneling and comfortable furniture and lots of bookshelves. The room was dominated by a fireplace at the far end. It wasn't lit, of course, but it seemed like the sort that would be very cozy in winter. On a table off to one side sat a big tray of Toll House cookies and a pitcher of milk, along with some glasses and small plates and paper napkins. A staircase with a carved banister led upstairs to where most of the guest rooms were.

Poole took the place in and immediately homed in on the cookies. He ate one in three bites, wiped his lips daintily, and then walked over to the male clerk seated behind the front desk. "Ms. Monique Forsythe's room, please. Augustus Poole calling. She is expecting me."

The young man consulted a list. "She's in room twelve. On the second floor. Up there." He pointed the way.

Poole followed the finger. When he saw that it directed him to the staircase, he was taken aback. He returned to the young man. "Isn't there an elevator?"

The desk clerk shook his head. "Sorry."

"Perhaps you could summon Ms. Forsythe for me?"

"We don't have phones in the rooms, sir. No televisions, either. People come here to get away from telephones and TVs."

"Then how was I able to speak to her earlier?"

"By phone?" The clerk tapped one on the counter near his elbow. "She probably used this. How long ago did you speak to her?"

"Perhaps an hour," said Poole.

"I was on my dinner break then, so I can't say for sure. But this is the phone that guests use, if they need one."

Poole turned to me. "Mr. Donne, would you be so kind as to go up and bring Ms. Forsythe down?"

"That won't be necessary," said a voice from the stairway.

Monique Forsythe stood on the landing halfway up to the second floor. The warm smile on her face suggested that whatever had transpired between her and Poole yesterday was water under the bridge. "Good evening, Gus," she said. "Good evening, Mr. Donne."

I returned the greeting, as did Poole. Ms. Forsythe descended the last few steps, walked over to the cookies, and put half a dozen on a plate. Then she poured two glasses of milk and turned to Poole. "Some for you, Gus?"

"Nothing, thank you. Mr. Donne—the other Mr. Donne, this Mr. Donne's father—prepared us a wonderful dinner earlier this evening."

"Are you sure you wouldn't like some cookies? They're very good."

"Perhaps just one—oh, dash it, why not two."

Ms. Forsythe added a couple more cookies to the pile on her plate, then moved back to the staircase. For the first time it occurred to me that she had a fine walk and an elegant posture. She started up the steps, paused, then regarded Poole over her shoulder. "Coming, Gus?"

Poole looked back at her, then shifted his view toward the top of the stairs. Then back to her. "Blast it," he said, heading for the stairs. And as he passed, so help me, he gave me a wink.

SINCE I WASN'T invited to whatever little gathering was taking place up in room twelve, I found a nice comfy easy chair and sat down to wait. I stared at the fireplace. I got up and took a cookie. They were probably for guests only, but nobody had said anything to Poole, so I figured it was okay. I sat back down and took a bite. Tasty, and still slightly warm from the oven. The chocolate chips had melted inside, the mark of a well-executed Toll House cookie.

When I'd finished it, I got up again and perused the bookshelves. An eclectic collection of literature lined the shelves, most of the stuff twenty or thirty years old, with a few semi-current self-help books, old *Sunset* magazines, and lots of Reader's Digest Condensed Books for good measure.

I found a fairly recent paperback titled *If I Never Get Back*, by a guy named Darryl Brock. It looked to be a story about a man who goes back in time to play with the old Cincinnati Red Stockings. I usually don't care much for baseball fiction, preferring instead the real thing. But this one sucked me right in; I was forty pages into it when I realized someone was standing in front of me.

I looked up. It was Monique Forsythe. She had a pack of cigarettes in her hand. Virginia Slims.

"Hello again, Mr. Donne," she said.

"Call me Jack."

"Jack, then. And I'm Monique. Gus would like you to join him upstairs. I'm going outside for a cigarette first, then I'll meet you up there."

While she headed outdoors, I got up and walked to the stairs. Halfway there I realized I still had the book in my hand. I took a quick look around, didn't see anyone watching, and stuffed it in my pocket.

I went down the second-floor hallway until I came to a room with a big 12 on the door. I knocked.

"It's not locked, Mr. Donne," said Poole. "Please come in."

I did. Inside, I found Poole and a woman who appeared to be in her early twenties. They sat in wooden chairs at a small wooden table.

Poole nodded a greeting. "Ah, Mr. Donne," he said. "May I present to you my daughter, Augusta?"

THE YOUNG WOMAN resembled Poole in no way I could determine. Her features were delicate, her nose and lips thin. Her hair was light brown in color and her eyes were gray. She was slender, about average height. And I could tell she'd recently been crying.

I crossed over to shake her hand. Whatever else she may have gotten from her father, she hadn't inherited his phobia about touching people, and she returned my grip with a nice firm one of her own.

"No doubt you're eager for an explanation," Poole said to me.

I looked around for another chair, didn't see one, then sat down on the edge of the bed. "I didn't know you had a daughter."

"Neither did I, Mr. Donne. Neither did I."

I said to Augusta, "Monique Forsythe is your mother?" When she nodded, I added, "And your father here just found that out tonight? He walked into the room and saw this lovely young woman sitting here with her mother, who said, 'Oh, by the way, here's the daughter you never knew you had'?"

"Oh, no," Augusta said. Her voice registered a bit lower than I expected, with no trace of any regional accent. "Mother told Mr. Poole about me yesterday. At the winery." Then to Poole, with the slightest bit of peevishness: "You didn't explain this to him?"

"How typically secretive of you, Gus," Monique said.

I turned to see her standing in the doorway. "Quick cigarette," I said.

"It didn't taste very good tonight, for some reason." She entered, closed the door, and came to sit beside me on the bed. "Gus has always been very closemouthed about his personal life. It's possible he had no intention of ever filling you in, so I will. I told him about Augusta yesterday, at Boot Canyon. I waited awhile, just chatting about old times, and then I told him."

"Old times?"

Poole interrupted. "Come, come, Mr. Donne, surely you deduced that I'd known Monique in the past. You asked me about it yourself. Miss Lubow suspected as well."

"I figured you knew her." I indicated Augusta. "Just not in the biblical sense."

"Things were much different in Boston in those days," Monique said. "We were young, we were carefree." A smile crept to her lips. "One of us was a lot skinnier."

"Two decades of the best of everything can put a bit of meat on a man's bones," Poole said.

"In any event, we were lovers," she continued. "We even had plans to—well, that doesn't matter now. Gus was the one to put an end to those plans."

"Really, Monique, Mr. Donne doesn't have to hear—"

She held up a hand to stifle him. "Anyway, eight months after the last time I saw him, Augusta was born."

I frowned. "If he bugged out on you, why did you name her after him?"

"To remind me never to trust any man again."

I looked at her. "And you haven't since?"

She laughed. "We all make many foolish decisions, especially when we're young. After Augusta was born I found several other men to trust, and then finally one to marry."

"Wait," I said. "You're married?"

"*Was.* My husband died a year ago. We had a very lovely time while he was alive." She looked wistful. "So it's not as if Augustus ruined me for other men, if that's what you're thinking." Another small laugh. "I couldn't very well change my daughter's name, could I? It's a nice, unusual name. It's served you well, hasn't it, dear?"

Augusta's laugh echoed her mother's, and I could see in her face that when she got older she would look exactly like Monique. Much better than looking like Poole.

"Most of the time it has," Augusta said. "But there was a period in grammar school when everyone knew they could make me mad by calling me 'Gus.' That wasn't very pleasant."

I said to Poole, "So. You two chatted about old times while the rest of us waited, and then you, Monique, very casually dropped it into the conversation. 'Oh, by the way, Gus, you have a twenty—' " Turning to Augusta: "What, twenty-one, twenty-two?"

"I'll be twenty-five next month."

Back to Monique, "So you said, 'You have a twenty-four-year-old daughter.' And you, Mr. Poole, did what?"

"I didn't believe her," he said. "After all, I hadn't seen the woman in two decades and—"

"Wait," I said. "You both travel in the same high-class food circles all this time, and you've never bumped into each other? Not even accidentally?"

"I've gone out of my way to avoid him," Monique said. "While she was growing up, Augusta never knew that my late husband wasn't her real father. I just thought it better that way. As far as she knew, we had been together for years before she was born."

Augusta chimed in. "Then when Father—that is, the man I've always thought of as my father—when he died, we were going through some old papers and—I found out the truth. I was very angry, for a time."

"She's quite the wildcat when she's angry," Monique said.

"If she's anything like her mother, I believe it," I said. "So. Augusta wanted to meet her real dad, and here came this perfect opportunity, what with you in NAMES and him being the speaker?"

"And it was handy, since the event was so near Santa Barbara. Just a hop, skip, and a jump from Los Angeles."

"And first chance you had, you dropped your little bombshell?"

"I actually intended to approach Gus before the dinner Wednesday night, but you arrived too late. Then I was going to speak to him Thursday morning, but poor Nicky Paoletti's death took care of that. I admit, when I finally got around to telling him, I didn't handle it very gracefully."

Poole's turn now. "As I was saying, at first I didn't believe a word of it. But Monique was quite persuasive. Eventually I did come to accept the truth of the situation."

"Then why the big blowup?" I turned to Monique. "Why'd you come storming out of there like a tornado?"

Augusta answered for her mother. "He refused to come and see me. He told Mother he'd lived blissfully for may years without a daughter, thank you very much, and he would be happy to live many years more without one. Mother practically begged him— but he still said no. That just made her more angry that she'd humiliated herself in front of him."

"I overreacted a bit," Monique admitted. "But it did pump a little life into that stuffy NAMES crowd, you must admit."

We talked well into the night. I found out that Augusta lived in Goleta, and that she'd gone to UC Santa Barbara, had a degree in communications, and was employed at the corporate office of a chain of health food stores, working on their marketing and advertising and such. I also gathered that her mother spent a lot of time in the Santa Barbara area because they enjoyed one another's company.

After a while the conversation turned from catching up on old times to the food business, and I began to tune out. Soon I was feeling drowsy again, so I excused myself and went back downstairs. I ate the last cookie and drank the last of the milk. Then I dove back into my baseball book.

I fell asleep in my chair and didn't awaken until I heard Poole harrumphing in front of me and telling me it was time to go home. I was too tired to do much more than drive, so I didn't bother asking about his sudden change of heart concerning Augusta. The only new information I gleaned was that Poole didn't much care for the Allman Brothers.

We got home at a quarter to three Saturday morning. Poole told me he expected us to proceed with our investigation into Paoletti's poisoning by eight-thirty. I assured him I'd be ready. Then I went to the guest room, where I got in bed and fell asleep instantly. Like the dead.

The knock on my door came at 7:58 A.M. I can pinpoint the time because when I heard the thumping my eyes popped open, and giant red numerals were staring me in the face. At first I couldn't divine what those numerals meant. Then I remembered I was in the guest room, which we'd furnished with the digital clock Jesus had given Dad as a Christmas present last year.

The numbers changed: zero, seven, five, nine. The knocking on the door came again—louder and more insistent. "Mr. Donne!"

I yelled back, "Yeah, yeah, I'm up!"

"No time to waste! We leave in thirty minutes!"

A tiny click. New red numbers now: an eight and three zeros.

A truly awful sound erupted from the clock's speaker, an old Abba song, "Fernando," in a cheesy synthesizer tone. Loud enough to wake the dead.

I NEARLY SCALDED myself in the shower. I cut myself shaving—not once but twice, cheek and chin. There wasn't any more of our recycled toilet paper on the roll, so I had to use a Kleenex, which made me feel as if I might be wasting precious natural resources. I silently cursed Augustus Poole, who would never run out of toilet paper since he had his own private roll.

I found him at the kitchen table. From the looks of things, he and my father were done with breakfast. They were deep in conversation about the virtues of various varieties of griddle cakes. Each had polished off a stack of Dad's buttermilk blueberry specials, along with glasses of orange juice and cups of coffee. I couldn't get over how well the two of them seemed to be getting along. Poole, the insufferable pain in the ass, interested only in proving himself the utmost authority on everything culinary—and now criminal—when he wasn't just stuffing his face. And my father, a man who suffered no fools gladly, down-to-earth, an okay cook but certainly nothing special, being built up as the hottest thing since Julia Child. Chattering and laughing together like old fraternity buddies.

Dad saw me standing in the doorway. "Hey, son. Get yourself some pancakes. There are a few left. I popped them in the oven to keep warm."

"Couldn't I have some fresh made?"

"I don't feel like cooking any more. The ones in the oven'll be fine, I'm sure."

Poole indicated his plate. "These were so tasty I'm sure even ones that have been drying out a little will meet with your approval."

Screw you both, I thought. I won't eat your damned leftovers. Instead I found a box of Wheaties. The latest umpteen-gazillion-dollar baseball sensation grinned out at me from the box. I grinned right back.

I went to the refrigerator for milk, but there wasn't any. No more fresh-squeezed orange juice, either. I dumped some prefab from a week-old carton, then dropped down at the end of the table to eat my Wheaties.

My father asked, "Why are you eating that cereal dry?"

"It's the latest thing. No milk to dilute the fiber content. Helps prevent cancer. Surely you knew about that, didn't you, Mr. Poole?"

I swear he was about to say yes, until he showed me a wise smile. "You are pulling my leg, aren't you?"

I smiled back. "Indeed I am."

They left me alone and chatted a while longer until Dad got up to go to the bathroom. As soon as he left, Poole turned to me. "Are we ready?"

"For what?"

"For the day's detecting. First you will take me to Ballard, where I will join the two Misses Forsythe, who have offered to conduct me on a sight-seeing tour. After I take my leave of them, I will begin my own inquiries. You will proceed to Rancho Calzada to speak to Roger Platt, in order to gather certain details concerning the late Mr. Paoletti. I have prepared a list of questions for you."

"What's Roger Platt doing at Rancho Calzada?"

"Evidently he persuaded Ted Taylor to let him prepare the NAMES banquet himself."

"He didn't say anything about that yesterday."

"The arrangement was made last evening. Mr. Platt has been lobbying for it since Thursday, but the Taylors were wary, as he has little reputation as a chef. By agreeing to bring his entire staff from the Courtyard Café, he broke down their defenses. Ms. Forsythe—the elder, that is—knew about this development almost as soon as it occurred. As I suspected, her finger is firmly on the pulse of all things epicurean."

"How lucky for me," I said. "I get to talk to Roger Platt again."

My sarcasm didn't seem to be affecting him anymore. "If time allows, when you finish with Mr. Platt you will question some of his staff. If not, we will just have to do without whatever intelligence might be gained by such interviews. It's more important for you to move on to Los Angeles, where I have a very full day lined up for you."

"You want me to go to Los Angeles? On a Saturday in the middle of the summer?"

"Is there something unreasonable about such a request?"

"It's hot. It's smoggy. There'll be traffic. All the tourists will be out. And I don't want to go. Isn't that enough?"

"But there are clues to be uncovered."

"If I'm down in L.A., who's going to be bodyguarding you?"

"Didn't we agree last night that I was no longer a target for murder? I'm dispensing with your services as a bodyguard. I feel quite safe without you. However, I wish to retain you as a private investigator. You are still on salary, as far as I'm concerned."

"Mr. Poole," I said. "Do you actually have some sort of plan? Or are we just going to keep talking to people until we find somebody who says, 'Oh, by the way, I poisoned Nicky Paoletti'?"

"Isn't it a well-known fact that most of what constitutes detective work is tedious drudgery?" He sounded as if he were lecturing me. "You are accustomed to such labor. Therefore you will engage in it on my behalf. I, meanwhile, will begin to put the clues together in order to uncover the perpetrator."

"You don't really believe that, do you?"

"I believe in myself. I always have. That is how I've managed to get where I am today. And that," he said, pushing away from the table, "is all I have to say on the matter. Please go and bring the car around. We are already behind schedule."

WE WERE NEARLY to Ballard when I asked, "So what changed your mind?"

"About what?"

"Meeting your daughter."

He took in a breath and exhaled slowly. "A fair question. With a rather simple answer. I needed to question her mother."

"Her mother?"

"Monique Forsythe knows everything about everyone in the restaurant world. I thought that, were I in her good graces, I could gather information that would aid you and me in our quest. Naturally, I would not be in her good graces were she still angry with me for failing to meet my daughter. Hence I agreed to the rendezvous last night. I must say, I plucked several gems from the conversation. I intend to gather more on our excursion today."

"Let me get this straight," I said. "You met your own daughter, for the first time in your life, simply because it would let you get information you couldn't get any other way?"

"That is an accurate statement."

"You wouldn't have gone to meet her otherwise?"

"That is correct."

"Mr. Poole?"

"Yes, Mr. Donne?"

"That is the single most coldhearted thing I have ever heard in my life."

He shrugged. "That is who I am. I do not have time for emotional entanglements. The people who inhabit the galaxy of wine and food are my true family. I am their benevolent patriarch, and they are my children. So it has been for many years, and so it shall ever be."

"Amen," I muttered.

"Excuse me?"

"Nothing," I said. The prick.

MONIQUE AND AUGUSTA Forsythe were waiting outside the Ballard Inn when we pulled up. Augusta had on a white sundress that made me long for the days when I was twenty-five years old and all girls looked as fresh-scrubbed and sexy to me as she did right now. Her mother wore a sleeveless blouse over a blue denim skirt. She had about an inch to go on her cigarette. She dropped the butt to the ground and stepped on it when she saw us. Still no move to pick it up. Damned litterbug.

Poole extracted himself from the car, and Augusta rushed up to give him a hug. He quickly held up his hands, palms out, to keep her back. She didn't seem the least put off.

Poole turned back to hand me three envelopes he produced from a pocket of his jacket. One had a big red number 1 on it, another a number 2, then number 3. "Number one is the list of questions I would like you to ask Roger Platt. Number two has the questions for his other employees, if time permits."

I started to open number one, but he made a gesture to halt me. "Please don't open it until you are in Mr. Platt's company. Spontaneity will aid your chances of his responding in kind."

"You mean if I don't know the questions beforehand, he won't know the answers beforehand?"

"Precisely."

"What half-assed private eye manual did you read that one in?"

He didn't bother to respond. Instead, he said, "Envelope number three is your list of destinations in Los Angeles."

"And when do I get to open that one? I don't want to drive to Hollywood and find you're sending me to a bunch of places in Orange County."

He seemed puzzled by this, chewing it over awhile. Finally he replied, "Very well. You may open envelope number three when you leave for Los Angeles. But not before."

He turned back to Monique and announced that it was time to leave. A red BMW was parked on the street in front of the B&B. Augusta climbed into the backseat. Watching Poole squeeze in, I considered giving him a kick in his fat rump as my contribution to the effort, but managed to resist the urge.

I returned to the Seville and took Route 246, heading east to Rancho Calzada. I found Joyce Taylor picking roses out front when I pulled up. She came over to greet me. "Hi, Jack. How are you holding up with Poole?"

I recounted a few of my tribulations, then told her about how Dad and Poole were becoming such good buddies. Poole was even building up Dad's culinary ego.

"Maybe we should have Ray come and be our chef tonight," Joyce said.

"I'm sure Roger Platt will do a fine job."

"I'm sure he will, too. But he's a bit of a pain. Don't tell Ted I said that. Actually, I just don't want him to worry that I think anything's wrong. He's stressing enough as it is."

"Still uptight about wanting to become a NAMESie?"

She nodded, making a face for a moment before bringing back a smile. "Come on, let's go inside."

As we walked toward the kitchen, Joyce was saying, "The thing is, Nicky Paoletti was in such total control in the kitchen. His confidence reassured Ted." She sighed. "Mr. Platt will probably work out fine. He's doing little of the actual cooking, after all. His pastry chef and all the other cooks are taking care of that. Which is how it would have been anyway. Whenever I was in the kitchen the other night, I never saw Nicky personally slaving over a hot stove. He mostly just flitted back and forth among the crew doing the real work, offering a comment here, taking a taste there. He orchestrated the meal more than he cooked it."

"That's what a lot of these big-dog chefs do," I said. I nodded in the direction of the kitchen. "Is Platt in there now?"

"He was fifteen minutes ago. I don't know where else he'd be. Why?"

"Poole wants me to talk to him."

"About what?"

I told Joyce about Augustus Poole, Detective. She thought it was the funniest news in the world. She was still chuckling as she walked off to put her roses in their vases.

Platt was indeed in the kitchen, hunching over a kettle of some steaming, brownish substance, mostly liquid. He had what appeared to be a recipe card in one hand. "I'd hate to have to start this all over," he was muttering as I walked up.

"Start what over?" I asked.

"This—oh, hello, Jack. This damned soup with okra and turnips. There's something not right about it."

I peered into the kettle. "May I?"

"Certainly."

I picked up a spoon and poked around until I rustled up a piece of something green I assumed was okra and something white that seemed to be turnip. I sipped the broth, then nibbled the morsels. "Seems fine to me," I said. "Kind of an odd taste, nothing I've ever had before. But I like it. What's wrong with it?"

"It's missing something. Though I'm certain all the proper ingredients are there."

"Maybe it just needs time for the flavors to meld."

"Maybe." He pouted. "I wish Nicky were here."

He got a faraway look in his eye, and I thought I saw a tear forming. "But he's not, is he?" Platt said. "And you know what? This morning was the first time I truly realized I was never going to see him again."

He took the spoon from me, tasted the soup, made a face. "More okra, maybe?"

"I don't know," I said. "A little okra goes a long way." I pointed my chin at the card in his hand. "That's the recipe?"

"One of Nicky's."

"May I see it?"

He handed over the card. Paoletti had written everything down in neat block capitals. All the ingredients, all the steps.

I gave back the card. "Joyce Taylor told me that Wednesday night Nicky wasn't directly involved in preparing most of the food. That he just oversaw everything."

Platt nodded. "He always had those dishes he prepared himself, but there were plenty of things on the menu at the café that Nicky trusted others with."

"Wouldn't he have wanted to save his personal best for this particular crowd tonight?"

Platt leaned forward conspiratorially, crooking a finger, drawing me near, and whispered, "Between you and me, many of those in this 'particular crowd' of so-called experts don't know their ass from their elbow when it comes to fine dining. A few of them do, but mostly they're only interested in seeing and being seen at the trendiest places." He frowned. "Still, I want the banquet tonight to be something special. I'm viewing it as—and this is utterly saccharine of me, but there you are—a tribute to Nicky. Not to attempt some of his signature dishes would be inappropriate, don't you think?"

"You put it that way, it seems like the right thing to do."

He smiled. "Was there something you wanted to see me about? I'm awfully busy."

I nodded. "You know about Augustus Poole's hiring me as a bodyguard this weekend, I'm sure. Now that it doesn't look like anyone's really after him—" I paused. "You heard about that business yesterday with his assistant?"

Platt nodded. "Quite a story. It was even on the news last night."

"I missed it. Anyway, since the bad guys were after her and not him, I've become a bodyguard without a body to guard. Now I'm doing whatever Poole asks me to do to earn my money. He's decided to play detective. He's given me a list of questions to ask you. Would that be okay?"

"I don't see why not. Just so it doesn't take too long."

I pulled out envelope number one, got a finger under the flap, and started to rip it open. "Haven't you seen the questions?" Platt asked.

"Poole wouldn't let me."

A small laugh. "I see. All right, fire away."

I scanned the list. It was written in tiny block lettering, similar to the late chef's. "Question one. Did you kill Niccolo Paoletti?"

"Of course not." He looked insulted.

"I'm sorry," I said. "We can stop this, if you want."

"It's all right. Go on."

"Okay, we've got two *a* and two *b*. Two *a* was if you answered yes to one." I gave him two *b*. "Do you know who did?"

"If I did, I would have told that police detective. I wish I did, but I haven't a clue."

"Question three. Do you know the names of any women Niccolo Paoletti may have been involved with?"

Platt giggled. "Surely *you* knew that Nicky and I used to— live together? That we split up a few months ago?"

I sighed. "I did, but Poole apparently didn't. Sorry." I glanced at the list. "Actually, this leads right into question four. Do you know of any *men* Niccolo Paoletti was involved with?"

He scowled. "He never brought any of his boyfriends home while he was living with me, if that's what you're asking."

"Sorry. Okay, number five. Did Niccolo Paoletti ever express any undue interest in 1947 Chateau d'Yquem sauternes?"

And so it went. The questions got sillier and sillier, and after two or three more I was too embarrassed to go on. If Poole demanded answers, I'd just make them up later.

I took my leave of Platt, thanking him for his time. Then I went out to the dining room, sat down at a table, and opened envelope number two. Inside was a virtual duplicate of the first list. Why couldn't Poole have told me to use the same list for Platt and anybody else I quizzed? Stupid question, one to which I'd probably never get an answer. He'd merely give me a pitying look and express doubts about my intelligence.

Then I spotted the Courtyard's hostess from lunch the day before, heading for the kitchen. I flagged her down and introduced myself. Her name was Wendy Spencer, and she was in her late twenties, I guessed. Tall, pretty. Hair still in a ponytail. A fresh-scrubbed look, just like Augusta.

I began to ask question number one, stopped, balled up the list, and shoved it into my pocket. I proceeded to quiz her in a more conventional manner, the questions flowing logically from one to another. And when I was done I knew no more about Nicky Paoletti than I had before.

Wendy told me she had a lot of work to do, so I let her go. Before she disappeared, she said, "Everybody at the café already talked to that Lieutenant Fitch. If you could track him down I'm sure you could save yourself some legwork."

"I'm sure I could," I said. "Thanks."

"You're welcome. And I hope you catch whoever did it. Nicky was a wonderful chef."

"We'll get whoever did it," I said. "Rest assured." But I was beginning to wonder.

endy Spencer was right. Why was I wasting my time asking these questions when Brad Fitch had talked to all the same people?

Why? Because Poole had sucked me in. And I'd fallen for it, simply because I felt a responsibility to earn my $4,500.

I went into Peter Taylor's office and called the Solvang substation. Fitch wasn't there. I paged him, then sat by the phone for fifteen minutes, leafing through a year-old *Wine Spectator*. I'd about given up on him calling me back anytime soon when the phone rang. I said hello, and he said, "Who's this?"

"It's Jack. We have to talk."

"What about? Your chubby buddy finally ready to confess?"

"You don't still think he might actually have done it?"

"You got a better candidate?"

"Maybe," I said. "A young lady by the name of Augusta Forsythe."

"No way, José."

"Why do you say that?"

"What is this, Twenty Questions? Whatever I found out about her is official police business."

"Since when are you so official with me?"

"Since you started spending twenty-four hours a day with my chief suspect."

"I'm not with him now."

"You're off the leash? How nice."

"Stop being an asshole, all right? I've got some information on Augusta Forsythe you may not have. Let's trade."

Silence from the other end of the line for a few seconds. Then: "Okay. Come on over and we'll have a chat."

"Where?"

"Solvang."

"They told me fifteen minutes ago you weren't there."

"I wasn't then, but now I am. You coming, or what?"

"I'm coming."

I hung up and checked my watch. Ten-thirty. What with my meeting Fitch and the weekend traffic I'd be sure to run into, I'd be lucky to get to L.A. by midafternoon. Swell.

I hopped in the car and drove to Solvang. Fitch was on the phone when I arrived. He motioned me to sit. The desk he was using was littered with bulging manila folders and used Styrofoam coffee cups. He got off the phone and said, "So talk."

"Augusta Forsythe is Augustus Poole's daughter," I said.

"You're kidding."

"It's true. She was even named after him."

The news surprised him. He shook his head. "Jeez. Frankly it's hard to imagine that guy ever actually having sex with anybody."

"He was a lot thinner then. Her mother is—"

"I know who her mother is. What do you think, I've just been sitting on my ass here? How do *you* know about this?"

I gave him the rundown of Poole's and my trip to the Ballard Inn the night before. Fitch processed the information, making notes as he went along. When I was done he said, "We checked out both women already, and they're both squeaky clean."

"How far back did you check?"

"Far enough. I also talked to Monique on Thursday morning. She didn't see anything or hear anything, just like the rest of those NAMES wackos. She didn't say anything about knowing Poole, but I didn't ask her if she did, either. I caught up with the girl yesterday afternoon. Same thing."

"So as far as you're concerned, you'd believe Poole did it before either of them did?"

"Jesus Christ, Jack. I don't necessarily think he did it. He's just my chief suspect because he had means, motive, and opportunity."

"Motive and opportunity I buy. But means? Okay, he had the wine, but what about the cyanide? You think he was just carrying it around in his pocket?"

"He could've been."

"But he also didn't have a motive until Wednesday night, after he and Nicky had their argument. Are you suggesting he was carrying around some poison on the off chance he'd get into a fight with somebody? Or that when he says he was scarfing chicken wings, he was really at the all-chemical supply store buying cyanide?"

"I was thinking maybe they already didn't like each other, long before Wednesday. Their argument was just another manifestation of that."

"Give me a break," I said.

"You asked."

I thought for a moment. "Look. Poole didn't do it. After being around him for three days, I know he wouldn't have wasted a bottle of the finest dessert wine in the world simply to knock someone off."

We went back and forth for another twenty minutes or so, Fitch trying to convince me Poole really was a likely suspect, me on the opposite side. While we were arguing I realized a significant fact. I didn't know *why* I was so convinced Poole hadn't done it. I just knew he hadn't.

Fitch told me he wanted to track down Poole and the two women, to question mother and daughter as to why they hadn't said anything during interrogation about their relationship to Poole. I told him they were gallivanting around Santa Barbara County playing tourist, and it might be difficult to find them. He asked if I knew what kind of car they were in. I said it was a blue Thunderbird. A rental.

Obstructing justice? Maybe. But this whole case had taken on such a weird rhythm, I felt I had to let things run their course. Poole's amateur methods were way too mystical for a pragmatist like me, but there you go. I'd made up my mind to do it his way.

I left Fitch, got back in the Seville, and headed for Highway 101 to start my trip south to L.A. I made good time until I got just outside of Thousand Oaks, at which point things ground to a virtual halt. Up ahead I could see the freeway narrowing to a single lane. A jackknifed semi blocked the others.

As my fellow drivers and I crept along, I pulled out envelope number three. I opened it and read what was inside.

Mr. Donne,

Please visit each of the restaurants on this list in order and find out what you can.

Sincerely,

Augustus Poole

There followed a list of eight, count 'em, eight establishments. I recognized the names of all but one. The ones I recognized were all pricy and fancy. I groaned out loud. How was I going to drop in on eight restaurants in one afternoon and still be back in Santa Ynez in time for the NAMES banquet tonight?

Maybe Poole just wanted me out of the way. Maybe he and his ex-lover and their daughter had been in on this together from the start, and they were getting me out of town as a means to cover their escape.

Red lights suddenly flashed ahead of me, and I narrowly avoided rear-ending a minivan. I told myself to pay attention to the road. After ten more exasperating minutes, I finally got past the accident and began to eat up the miles to L.A.

I DROVE WEST on Olympic Boulevard, heading for the first place on Poole's list. Fanucci's was on the ground floor of an office building a half mile west of the San Diego Freeway. You entered the restaurant through a tiny lobby just big enough for the reservations stand, the maître d' manning it, and one or two customers. Then you passed through a gorgeous bar, done up in cherry wood and etched glass. You could eat in the bar, at one of five tables and an equal number of booths, or move all the way through to the main dining room beyond.

It was already three o'clock when I got there. I stood in the alcove, waiting to see if someone would take notice. After about half a minute someone did—a stocky guy with a round face, wearing a sport coat and dress shirt and slacks but no tie. "May I help you?" he asked.

"I've only got a few hours to spend here in L.A., and an acquaintance of mine has been after me to come here for ages. I thought while I was in town, I'd take advantage of the opportunity. Is the kitchen open?"

"I'm afraid not," he said. "We only serve lunch on Saturdays till two-thirty."

I looked crestfallen. "Oh."

"Who's your friend?"

"Nicky Paoletti."

He looked stricken. "Nicky?"

I let a confused face overtake the hangdog one. "Is something the matter?"

He gave me a deeply sympathetic look. "You mean to say you don't know?"

"Know what?"

"I have some very bad news."

"Bad news?"

He nodded. "Nicky . . . Nicky's dead."

"Dead?"

"He died two nights ago. God, I feel just awful having to be the one to tell you."

I made myself look flabbergasted. "How did he—?" I waved a hand in the air, as if I couldn't bring myself to say the last word.

"Die? Apparently he drank some poisoned wine intended for somebody else. I can't believe you haven't heard about this. It's been all over the papers and TV."

"I don't own a television. And I've been having a bit of a disagreement with my paperboy."

He looked me over as if trying to figure out if I could possibly be for real. He decided I was. "Tell you what. I'll cook you up something myself, if you don't mind eating it at the bar. And also if you'll have a drink with me."

"I guess I could use a drink. This is a terrible shock."

"No doubt." He held out a hand. "Bill Fanucci."

We shook. "Jack Fitch." I indicated the surroundings. "Are you *the* Fanucci?"

"That I am. Come on in and have a seat."

We went into the bar, and I sat down on a leather stool. Fanucci raised a hinged partition, crossed through, and leaned on the polished wood surface across from me. "What'll it be?"

"What are you having?"

"Bourbon and soda."

"Sounds good."

While he was making our drinks, he asked, "How do—*did* you know Nicky?"

"I've eaten at the Courtyard Café many times, whenever I'm in Montecito. After the fourth or fifth time, I just had to meet the chef."

He handed me my drink and raised his own. "To our late friend."

"To Nicky." We clinked our glasses together and sampled our drinks.

"I mix a hell of a drink, if I say so myself," Fanucci said. "But I'm not a half bad cook, either. Why don't I just scout around the kitchen and whip something up for you? Anything you don't eat?"

"I eat everything."

"Good. I'm so blasted tired of these people who don't 'touch' things. Vegetarians, low-fat people, people who won't eat wheat or drink milk. They're just infuriating." He paused. "I'll be right back. If anyone comes in, tell them to wait. Or tell them to go to hell. It's up to you."

He disappeared through a swinging door. I waited. No one came in, so I didn't get to exercise my prerogative. After ten minutes or so Fanucci came back, told me it'd be another ten, and vanished again. After the allotted time he returned, bearing a huge plate of pasta heaped with clams, shrimp, and vegetables.

"This looks wonderful," I said sincerely.

"Like I told you, I'm not a bad cook. Not like Cesar, though."

"Your chef?"

He nodded. "The man is an absolute master in the kitchen. He can whip together food that literally melts in your mouth."

I took a bite of my pasta. It was tasty—not great, but okay. It was probably wise that Fanucci had Cesar around.

"This is terrific," I said, forking another bite. "So tell me how you know Nicky."

"It's a very incestuous business, if you get my drift," Fanucci said. "Everybody knows everybody. But Nicky *really* knew everybody. He was friendly with just about every important restaurateur in southern California." He paused. "I'd known him for years. Before I found Cesar, I even tried to get him to come to work here. But he didn't want to live in a big city. He was very happy up there in the boondocks of Santa Barbara. He enjoyed being a big fish in a small pond. But let me tell you, he could have been a big fish in *any* pond."

I kept eating, and Fanucci kept talking. He drifted off the topic of Nicky Paoletti after a while and on to the restaurant business in general. Before I knew it, the clock had passed four. I still had seven restaurants to go.

Having finished my pasta, I excused myself to go to the rest room. When I came back, I pulled out my wallet and said, "So what do I owe you?"

Fanucci held up a hand and shook his head. "Not a cent. It was in honor of Nicky. How could I possibly charge you?"

"That's very sweet of you. I promise I'll do my best to stop in again next time I'm in town."

"You do that, Jack."

On my way out I checked my wallet and found out it was a good thing he hadn't charged me. All I had was a ten-dollar bill.

Which meant I would have had to put my lunch on a credit card—one that said Jack Donne, not Jack Fitch. My undercover skills had obviously eroded since my days with BATF, and I resolved to retire my alias right then and there. Good plan, Jack, I said to myself.

I got back to the car and took another look at Poole's list. Five of the seven remaining restaurants were in the West Side area, one was downtown, and one was in Encino, in the San Fernando Valley. I figured I'd hit the five nearest to me, then if there was time head downtown and finally catch the place in Encino on my way north.

Then I realized how stupid an idea that was. In order to be back in time for the banquet, which started at 8:00 P.M., I had to be home by seven if I was going to wash up and change clothes. I supposed I could just show up on time dressed the way I was, grungy from driving around all day. But even if I did that, I'd have to leave L.A. by 6:00 P.M. at the latest. Which meant I had less than two hours to make my rounds.

By the time I found an open ATM and replenished my cash supply, I was down to an hour and a half. The closest place on my list to Fanucci's was Le Livre Ouvert on Gayley Avenue in Westwood. I found a parking spot around the corner, made my way to the restaurant, and entered.

"May I help you, m'sieur?" asked a short, swarthy guy in a

tuxedo. He was lurking in the foyer. He eyed my faded polo shirt and jeans with oily displeasure.

"I hope so. I'm Jack Donne of Donne Vineyards."

"Yes?"

"Donne Vineyards? You have our chardonnay on your wine list?"

"Yes?"

"I happened to be in the neighborhood, and I thought I'd stop by and see how my wine was doing. Maybe talk to somebody about adding a little more of our product?"

"You would have to see our Mrs. Clayton about that. She is very busy now preparing for the evening's repast, and I'm afraid you won't—"

"Give it a rest, will you, Henri?"

The woman who burst into our conversation was built like Mae West, and she sounded a little like her too. She was somewhere in the vicinity of seventy years old, had on a little too much makeup, and her hair was a shade of brassy blond not found in nature. But she was dressed classily in an off-white pants suit over a pale blue blouse of what looked to be pure silk.

Henri sputtered, "But, Mrs. Clayton—"

"Can it." She turned to me. "Henri thinks just because the place has a French name we've all got to act snooty. I'll let you in on a secret. Henri's real name is Henry, and he's never been closer to Paris than Hoboken."

"You wound me, Mrs. Clayton," said Henri.

"Sure I do." She held out a hand to me. "Jane Clayton. Glad to meet you, Mr. Donne. I know your father and your uncle."

I shook her hand. "Nice to meet you, Mrs. Clayton."

"Jane."

"Jane, then. I'm Jack. I had other business in town, and I

thought I'd drop by and check up on your wine cellar, if that's okay."

"The cellar's fine. We sell a fair amount of your chard. Actually, it's funny you should show up on my doorstep, because we're looking to get some more."

"I'm happy to hear it."

I may have been talking about wine, but I was thinking about how to get the conversation around to Nicky Paoletti. I took stock of the woman I was talking to, decided what the hell, and made a snap judgment. "Jane, is there somewhere we can speak privately?"

"Come on to my office." She glanced past my shoulder. "What are you looking at, Henri? Go polish the silver or something." Back to me. "This way, Jack."

We made our way to her office. She directed me to a small sofa, while she sat down in a leather executive's chair behind a big desk. "What can I do for you?" she asked.

"You heard about what happened to Niccolo Paoletti, didn't you?"

"Poor Nicky. Everyone in the restaurant business has heard. Terrible, just terrible." She sniffed. "I also heard the cops think Augie Poole did it."

"Augie?"

"That's what a lot of people call him behind his back. Why, what do you call him?"

"Mostly 'Mr. Poole.' He calls me 'Mr. Donne.' "

She made a face. "You look like a sensible young man. What in God's name are you doing associating with that old buffalo?"

I told her my story—or as much of it as I thought I needed to. She was acquainted with Monique Forsythe, of course, and knew Monique had a daughter, but had never met Augusta. I left out naming Augusta's father. When I was finished, Jane said, "So you don't believe Augie did it?"

"No, I don't. I'm trying to find out who did. Can you think of anything that might help me?"

She pondered awhile. "I really can't. As far as I knew, Nicky was happy as a clam up there. I mean, he irritated a lot of people— he had a very irritating personality sometimes. But—"

She paused. "There was one thing. I heard this fourth- or fifth-hand, so don't put too much credence in it. Supposedly there was a time in the not-so-distant past Nicky thought he ought to be getting more money from Roger Platt or a partner-ship or some damn thing. He threatened to stage a one-man strike if he didn't get his way."

"What happened?"

"Roger caved in." She shrugged. "If you knew all the goofy rumors that float around the restaurant trade—"

She was starting to look a little antsy. I wasn't quite done, though. "I know you're busy, and I don't want to keep you, but just one more thing. Did you ever hear any talk of Nicky going to work for somebody else?"

She smiled and shook her head. "Honey, you hear that crap all the time. If you believe a tenth of it, you're going to be wrong way more often than you're right."

OUT ON THE street again, I checked my watch. Five-twenty. I thought for a moment I would try one more place, then head for home. Then I realized I didn't have the time. I really did need to clean up before making my appearance at Rancho Calzada; otherwise nobody would want to sit by me.

It took ten minutes to get on the 405 Freeway, and another ten to get to the top of the Sepulveda Pass. A two-mile-long line of cars waiting to get onto the Ventura Freeway greeted me. This was not good, since I too had that particular route in mind.

I drove along an inside lane all the way down the hill, cut in front of a Toyota Celica whose driver honked at me, then slid in front of a pickup truck whose driver gave me the finger. And saved a good ten minutes.

Once I negotiated the interchange and hit the northbound Ventura, it was smooth sailing. The Seville maintained a steady eighty miles per hour all the way, with occasional bursts of higher speed as I passed somebody. I zoomed through the San Fernando Valley, then on past Thousand Oaks and Camarillo, past Oxnard and Ventura, and on into Santa Barbara. Here the traffic screeched to a stop.

This time the big rig was on the northbound side. It took me fifteen minutes to go one mile, before I could get off the freeway and zigzag via surface streets to the 154. After all that, I still managed to pull into our drive at home just a few minutes past seven-thirty.

Dad awaited me in the house, wearing a gray suit and a tie. I quizzed him with a look, and he said, "Augustus invited me to the NAMES banquet. He said for me to catch a ride with you."

I didn't have time to argue with him. As I headed for the bathroom, stripping off my clothes, I asked, "Any calls?"

"Just Augustus, five or six times. And Maggie, twice."

"Where is the Great One, anyway?"

"Already at the Taylors'. He wanted you to call him the instant you got in."

"Why didn't he just call me on the car phone?"

"I didn't ask."

I detoured into my office, found Rancho Calzada's number, and punched it in. It took a few minutes for the guy who answered to track down Poole. "Did you have a fruitful afternoon, Mr. Donne?" he asked.

"Moderately. Why don't I tell you all about it when I see you? It won't take me long to clean up. We should be there in forty-five minutes."

"The banquet is scheduled for eight o'clock."

"I know that. I was running around with your errand list, remember? Have them save some of the first course for us, okay?"

"I shall not permit them to begin until you and your father arrive. You are my associate, and your father is my friend, and I would not wish you to miss any of the proceedings."

"That's mighty big of you, Mr. Poole."

"Is that a pun?"

"Not at all. I'll get off now and just fill you in when I get there."

"That will be acceptable. Although I hardly need to learn the results of your endeavors."

"Why's that?"

"Because," he said. "I already know who killed Niccolo Paoletti. And that person is not going anywhere."

oole's statement wasn't as major a revelation as it might have been, since on the drive back from Los Angeles I'd also come up with a pretty good idea who was responsible for poisoning Nicky Paoletti. A quick shower and shave, some minor speeding, and Dad and I made it to Rancho Calzada in thirty-five minutes. I gave Dad a brief rundown on the way over. His only comment was "I'll just be glad when these maniacs are out of my valley."

The dining room at Rancho Calzada was festive, to say the least. Each table was laid with fine china, sterling silver, and expensive crystal. The centerpieces were maybe a bit much—flowers and ferns and something I guessed to be rosemary bursting out at all angles, almost dangling into some folks' plates.

The crowd was restless. The NAMES members milled around their tables. Many had drinks in their hands. A quick scan of the room showed me that several had been hitting the bar with vigor.

Dad and I found Poole near the dais, engaged in conversation with Roger Platt. "The turnips will turn," Platt was saying as we walked up.

"Nonsense, Mr. Platt. I am an authority on soups, and a little extra time spent in the kettle won't hurt."

Platt seemed about to disagree when he noticed me standing there. "Hello, Jack. Look, Mr. Poole, he's here. Can my people please start serving now?"

Poole nodded a greeting to my father and me. "The two Mr. Donnes. How pleasant to see you both. Please take your seats. I've chosen places for you at a table of honor." He chuckled. "Perhaps not *the* table of honor; that is where I will be. But I have arranged some interesting company for you."

He pointed off to the left of the dais, to a table with a big number 2 in blue on a gold placard. Monique Forsythe stood by the table, wineglass in hand, wearing a black dress that revealed some cleavage. Her daughter Augusta was already sitting down, wearing a white off-the-shoulder dress that was also very flattering. Across the table from Augusta, seemingly engaged in conversation with her but simultaneously checking out everyone in the room—ever-watchful, ever-vigilant—was Brad Fitch.

I indicated Fitch and said to Poole, "What's he doing here?"

"I convinced the lieutenant it would be in his best interest to attend."

"And he just accepted that?"

"His exact words were 'I'm going to give you enough rope to hang yourself, Mr. Poole. Then I'm going to kick your horse myself.' Who would have thought him capable of such a picaresque turn of phrase?"

"That's Brad," I said. "Picaresque as the day is long."

"Indeed."

Poole motioned us to our table, then lumbered to the dais. Roger Platt scurried off to the kitchen. Standing at his place on the dais, Poole tinked on his water glass with a butter knife. "My friends!" he boomed to the multitude. "Let the banquet begin!"

Everyone found their seats. Monique Forsythe sat down to her daughter's right. My father, who had walked over and introduced himself to the Forsythe women, was on Augusta's left. I took a chair between Dad and Fitch. It still left our table with a couple of empty seats.

As I dropped down into my place, I said to the lieutenant, "What's a nice guy like you doing in a place like this? You just taking the opportunity to view all your suspects together at one time?"

"What makes you think all my suspects are here?"

"I figure you wouldn't like it if anybody slipped through the cracks. You still think Poole did it?"

"I'll let you know."

A squad of waiters and waitresses emerged from the kitchen. Wendy Spencer herself headed for our table, carrying a big tureen on a tray. Hostess, waitress, she did it all. She dished the soup into our bowls, which were made of some of the finest, whitest porcelain I'd ever seen, with two narrow rings of gold a quarter inch or so down from the rim.

A busboy was on Wendy's heels, handing out fresh-baked rolls. I spied on my tablemates as they sipped their soup. Dad seemed impressed, Monique Forsythe less so. Augusta squinched up her face and said, "Are these turnips? I hate turnips."

I tasted my soup. The flavors had indeed melded since that morning. It was good—not something you'd write home about, though. I wondered if Platt had gone on with his original batch or started over.

The whole room was chowing down. I managed to catch a few snatches of conversation—one guy was talking about Il Something-or-other in Rome, where the olives were heavenly. A woman who'd fawned over Poole at her interview Thursday afternoon was babbling something about Bustamente. I didn't know if it was a wine, a cheese, or a restaurant, but whatever it was, it was heavenly, too. Everything was heavenly. I was heavenly. Poole was heavenly. The whole universe was positively heavenly.

Up on the dais Poole held court among the same group he'd sat with on Wednesday night. He alternated sips of soup with pronouncements on the woeful state of gourmet dining. He was in his element, the center of attention at perhaps *the* epicurean event of the year.

The soup was soon gone, but salad followed. When it arrived, Fitch peered at his plate and said, "The places I usually go, you get soup *or* salad. Not both."

It was a nice salad, but again by no means heavenly, at least not to my semi-trained palate. I counted four different kinds of lettuce, two of which I'd actually eaten before. Bits of pecan and hearts of palm, some tiny round things that may have been peas, shaved cheese of unknown origin on top, a dressing that reminded me of mustard and mint, although I think neither was actually present. The dressing was just a bit too thick for me.

As I felt somewhat responsible for his being there, I was relieved that Fitch managed to behave himself through the first two courses. I caught him eyeing both Forsythe women as well as Poole, but he refrained from questioning anybody. I decided that he was lying in wait for someone, probably Poole, to slip up and expose guilt. At which point Fitch could pounce and put him away with the least possible effort.

Third course. Fitch was obviously expecting an entrée, and he was suitably impressed when Wendy placed an individual casserole dish before him. He leaned over to me. "I'm kind of hoping we don't catch whoever did it tonight. I think I may be too stuffed to put the cuffs on 'em."

It was the first dish I was genuinely impressed with: thin

slices of some as-yet-unidentifiable meat layered with equally thin slices of potato—a spicy, succulent casserole. "Anybody know what this is?" I asked.

"It's called Canard et Pommes de Terre Nicky," Wendy said. " 'Duck and Potatoes Nicky.' "

Uh-oh, I thought.

"Is this *duck?*"

It was loud, and it was Poole. He was standing up at his place, glaring down at the dish before him.

"Yes, sir," said his waiter. "Canard et pommes—"

"I am allergic to duck!" Poole roared. "Any fool who's read a line of my work would know that! Is someone trying to poison me?"

He turned toward the kitchen and shouted, "Mr. Platt!"

Platt burst out of the kitchen as if someone had lit his pants on fire. He rushed up to the dais, making little calming-down motions. "I had no idea, Mr. Poole. You have no idea how sorry I am." He whisked the plate away and handed it to a passing busboy. "Please let me prepare something else for you."

"It's too late for that," snapped Poole. He made an angry gesture in the direction of our table. "Sit down, Mr. Platt."

Platt did as ordered, taking the empty seat next to Brad Fitch. A tense silence settled over the room, as if someone had dropped a curtain. Poole remained standing, all eyes on him.

He cleared his throat. "I intended to save what I had to say this evening until after dessert. I apologize, but for me this meal is ruined. Therefore I will make my speech now. I beg everyone's indulgence, and if you feel you must continue eating while I speak, I shall not be insulted."

He paused for a swallow of wine, then went on. "I barely knew Niccolo Paoletti, and in the short time we were acquainted, I'm afraid we got off on the wrong foot. Nevertheless, I knew his reputation, and I respected that. An esteemed member of our community is gone, and we must face that loss. None of us more so than Roger Platt."

He gestured to our table. "Mr. Platt," Poole continued, "has suffered more than any of us. He has lost not only a fine chef but a great and good friend. And since I intend to make my address tonight a kind of memorial to Niccolo Paoletti, I feel it only appropriate to name the individual responsible for his untimely demise."

A collective sharp intake of breath. I checked my tablemates. We all traded puzzled looks.

"There is a reason this subject is close to my heart," Poole was saying, "for I myself have been under suspicion. I have been singled out for persecution simply because I was unfortunate enough to discover Mr. Paoletti's corpse. Oh, perhaps our little contretemps contributed in some small way to the black cloud that seems to have fallen over me—"

"Oh, please," said Monique Forsythe.

"—but in large part it is a web of circumstantial evidence that has placed a shadow over my head."

Some oohs. Some aahs. He had the whole room in the palm of his chubby hand.

"But no matter. I can take the heat. I can stay in the kitchen."

Fitch whispered out of the side of his mouth, "You ask me, he's stayed in there a lot longer than he should've."

Poole: "I can roll with the punches, and I can—"

Monique Forsythe could stand it no more. She got up from her chair. "Enough with the clichés, Gus. Can you please just get on with it?"

Poole threw her a stern look that gave no evidence of the two of them having palled around most of last night and today. "Very well, Monique," he said. To the throng: "I have solved the murder of Niccolo Paoletti, and the murderer is in this very room!"

That got everyone going again, half the people in the room eyeing the other half with deep misgiving. "Let us go back in time," Poole said. "Not quite so far as Wednesday night, when the actual murder was committed, but rather to Thursday afternoon. If you recall, at that time I interviewed many of you about your knowledge concerning the death of Mr. Paoletti. I was laboring under the misconception that several attempts had been made upon my life. The contamination of the bottle containing my rare and precious 1947 Chateau d'Yquem sauternes was viewed as another such attempt. I felt my very existence was in danger. Interrogating the members of NAMES was an attempt to protect myself. I had my bodyguard, Mr. Donne, but he could not possibly attend to me every second. Proactive behavior was indicated."

Heads nodded around the room. Whatever Poole said was okay by them.

"I discontinued my interviews after meeting with Monique Forsythe, over there. That episode ended badly. For subjecting you all to that scene, I humbly apologize. I am sure Ms. Forsythe does as well."

The crowd turned as one to scrutinize her. "Fine," she said after a suitable pause. "I'm sorry to have put you delightful people through such psychic trauma."

"Good," Poole said. "Now we can proceed. It matters little what caused the blowup of which I just spoke. Suffice to say that, with several NAMES members still uninterrogated, I felt a certain discomfort."

Both Forsythes rankled at the "matters little" part, and who could blame them? The elder of the two seemed on the verge of another outburst. I caught her eye and whispered,

"Don't bother. He's on a roll." She pursed her lips, nodded, and remained silent.

Poole was shifting into high gear. "Then, on Thursday night, something happened that shook me to my very core. My trusted associate, my personal assistant Carla Lubow, appropriated a vehicle belonging to Mr. Donne here and started off for parts unknown. Although assuming the appearance of one who believed her rather questionable story, I was on the alert. I now had to question whether anything was as it seemed. Could it be that Miss Lubow had arranged the attempts on my life? That *she* had slipped poison into my bottle of wine, perhaps to gain revenge for some imagined slight? And that now, either racked with guilt or fearing discovery, she was attempting to escape into the night?"

I surveyed the room again. All present continued to be enraptured with Poole. Even the service people who had come out from the kitchen were caught up in his spell.

Poole went on, "Then on Friday morning occurred the most disturbing event yet. I was rousted from a sound sleep by the sudden appearance of Lieutenant Bradley Fitch."

Poole indicated Fitch, and the assembled masses turned to view the infidel. "The lieutenant had come to take me to a police station," Poole said. "Evidence had been uncovered that the poisoned wine could not possibly have been an attempt on my life. Although wisely refraining from placing me under arrest, the lieutenant subjected me to a humiliating series of questions, lasting several hours." A small exaggeration—I let it go, and so did Fitch. "I was being treated as a common criminal, and I must tell you, my friends, I did not enjoy it one bit."

He paused to wet his whistle again. "Fortunately, Mr. Donne managed to find suitable counsel for me, and I escaped from this harrowing experience with my freedom. But I was badly shaken, and for the moment I could no longer concentrate on the investigation. I allowed Mr. Donne to drive me to Santa Barbara, where we had lunch at Mr. Platt's establishment. Being in a place so influenced by Mr. Paoletti made me realize that, although the poisoned wine was not a direct attempt on my own life, it could be an attempt to strike at me in another way. The perpetrator would see me convicted of murder, and the state of California would unwittingly carry out his desires and put me to death. And ultimately, if this heinous plan succeeded, at midnight some dark and stormy evening Augustus Poole would die in the gas chamber for a crime he did not commit. And, irony of ironies, the agent of death would be cyanide gas!"

He had himself wound up now. Beads of sweat rimmed his forehead. Michael Gottberg rose to offer him assistance, but Poole shook him off. Gottberg returned to his seat.

Poole smiled to the assembly to show he was all right, then went on. "Something happened that turned the entire matter upside down. I trust you all have heard or read about the events that took place on a narrow country road a bit south of here. With the assistance of Mr. Donne and some worthy agents of the U.S. Customs Service, I escaped another hair-raising encounter. But Miss Lubow—the true target of one of my 'murder attempts'— was taken into custody. A lesser man would have been relieved to learn that no one was actually seeking to end his life. But not Augustus Poole. I resolved at that moment to solve the murder of Niccolo Paoletti, thus removing all shadow of suspicion from myself and letting Mr. Paoletti's spirit move on to its final resting place for all eternity."

"Amen," Monique Forsythe and I muttered under our breath, simultaneously.

"But how to accomplish that?" Poole continued. "I decided

to play all the cards that were available to me. If you will think back to the events of Thursday afternoon—"

"This guy should have brought along a blackboard," Fitch whispered.

"—you will remember the incident with Ms. Forsythe. I needn't bore you with details. She wanted to meet with me privately about a matter of mutual interest. At the time, wrapped up in what I thought were attempts on my life, I could not agree to do so. But now, with the outcome of the case on the line, I had to change my mind. Ms. Forsythe, as most of you know, possesses a vast knowledge of the restaurant world. I had to gain her confidence, so that I could subtly question her in hopes of gaining some clue to the identity of the murderer."

Monique jumped to her feet, furious. "You fat bastard! Are you saying you only met with Augusta and me so you could pick my brain?"

An anxious murmur filled the room. "I'm afraid so, my dear," Poole said.

She looked as if she might be ready to strangle him. "Come on, Augusta. We're leaving," she said, moving to help her daughter up.

Fitch growled. "You're not going anywhere."

"I beg your pardon?"

"No one's leaving this room until we get this mess sorted out. You might as well sit yourself back down in your chair till he's finished."

"You can't make me stay."

"I've got a badge that says I can. And if that isn't enough, I've got a whole squad of deputies posted around all the exits."

That convinced her. She resumed her seat. Poole had taken advantage of the brief break to refresh his batteries, and he stood on the dais again, as full of himself as ever. "I apologize for the interruption, and I promise it will not happen again."

He paused, as if making up his mind how to say what he wanted to say. "By synthesizing all the information at my command, I came to one inescapable conclusion. The person who killed Mr. Paoletti was merely using murder as a means to a completely different end. The real target, and this illustrates the utter nefariousness of the plot, was—Augustus Poole."

Another round of oohs and aahs.

"Carefully gathering facts, via interviews and numerous telephone calls, I could find no evidence that anyone existed who might have sufficient reason to murder Mr. Paoletti. But I did find irrefutable evidence that a certain person would gladly do away with an innocent man in order to get back at me. What I viewed earlier as mere misdirected suspicion was actually a deliberate attempt to frame me for Niccolo Paoletti's murder."

All of a sudden I didn't care for the direction he was heading, but like Fitch I was willing to let him have his rope. He took a bit more of it.

"Who could this person be? One thing the interviews on Thursday taught me was that certain people bore grudges about criticisms written long in the past. Ladies and gentlemen, I am an unbiased reviewer. If something is good, I praise it. If something is unsatisfactory, I report that. There is no rancor involved."

He leaned forward toward the crowd. "But some of you cannot forget perceived injustices and some of your long memories could be dangerous. For instance—"

His first example was off-putting. "You, Mr. Donne." He was pointing at my father. "I discovered you were upset about a review of your wine several years ago. You could have taken this opportunity to exact revenge."

"That's the stupidest thing I've ever heard," Dad said.

"Having spent time in your presence, and enjoying your fine

cooking and hospitality, I do find it an unlikely scenario. Let us move on. It could have been *you*, Arthur Benedict."

The elderly southern gentleman eased back in his chair and chuckled. "It's an honor being selected by you, Mr. Poole, but I'm a little too old to be getting mixed up in this sort of thing."

Poole nodded. "Agreed. Then perhaps *you*, Stella O'Neill?"

All heads swiveled to the table in the back where the woman from Miami sat. "That's right, Mr. Poole, I did it. I also shot JFK and Cock Robin too."

"No need to be snippy, Mrs. O'Neill. I don't suspect you in the slightest. I'm merely using you as an example to show the number of people who might misconstrue the intent of my writings. Let me choose another." He looked down the dais. "What about you, Ted Taylor?"

Ted said, "Huh?"

"You were terribly upset about a review lo these many years ago. So you arranged to have the NAMES meeting here, on your very own premises, where it would be easy to send someone in to take back my Chateau d'Yquem as I slept, put in some poison, and force Niccolo Paoletti to drink it."

"Are you insane?" Ted asked.

"Did you?"

"Certainly not!"

Poor Ted. He wanted badly to lash back at Poole, but he was still so caught up in joining this group of wackos that he couldn't bring himself to call the man a twenty-four-karat idiot to his face.

Poole said, "Of course, I have no such belief. Merely another example for you all to consider." He brought up a hand to rub his chin, as if to aid his thinking. "No, Mr. Taylor is not the culprit. But now, after long and hard consideration, I will tell you who is."

"Please do," Fitch whispered. "My backside is starting to get numb."

"The person attempting to frame me for murder had been prompted by one of my reviews. But—and this is what made the process of discovery so difficult, what taxed my brain to such a degree—it is not a review that has appeared in my newsletter. Neither is it a review that has appeared in the *Chronicle*, or in *Bon Appetit*. It is not a review that has appeared at all. Ladies and gentlemen, I am being framed for the murder of Niccolo Paoletti because of a review that has not yet been written!"

A whole new level of hubbub filled the room. Several people at the back tables stood up so as to better view the next exciting revelation.

They were quickly rewarded. Poole pointed a meaty finger at my table and said, "*You* are the murderer, Roger Platt. You suspected I would write a negative account of my meals here at the NAMES convention, and you decided to cut off any bad publicity before it occurred! So you poisoned your chef and left clues that would incriminate me! Oh, what a tangled web you weave!"

Platt was instantly on his feet. "That's the most ridiculous thing I ever heard!" His face was bright pink, and the veins stuck out in his neck.

Poole said, "It was you, was it not, who talked poor Mr. Paoletti into requesting me to share my bottle of Chateau d'Yquem?"

"I wasn't even here that night. I was at my restaurant all evening."

"You could have spoken to him before he left to come here. You could have put the bug in his ear, knowing that given his Italian temper, his request would result in an incriminating argument with me—"

Time to make my move. "Hold on, Mr. Poole," I called. "Before you dig yourself any deeper a hole than you've already got."

I stood up. Poole glared at me. I ignored him and addressed the crowd. "I hate to have to be the one to tell everybody, but Mr. Poole has made a little mistake. Roger Platt didn't kill Nicky Paoletti because he was trying to incriminate somebody else."

My turn for some oohs and aahs. Poole said, "Mr. Donne, you're embarrassing yourself *and* me. The first lesson a detective must learn is that the most obvious answer is nearly always the right one. You told me that yourself. Given that Mr. Paoletti was the intended victim all along, and given that he was, by all accounts, much beloved in the restaurant community, the only possible person who would have the least interest in killing him is Roger Platt."

"Oh, I agree with you there, Mr. Poole," I said. "You just got his motive wrong, that's all."

Poole looked puzzled. I turned to Platt. "Where were you around two o'clock this past Thursday morning?"

Steam was coming out of his ears. "Not you, too. I've told the police a dozen times." To Fitch: "Sir, do I really have to respond to such an absurd accusation?"

"Just answer the question," Fitch said.

"Very well." Back to me. "I was home. In bed. Asleep."

"Can you prove that?"

"No, I cannot. I was alone." He glared at me. "Can *you* prove where you were at that time?"

"Probably," I said. "But then, I'm not a murderer. How long has Nicky been looking to go out on his own?"

"What in heaven's name are you talking about?"

I faced the crowd. "How many of you in this room in the last six months had been approached by Nicky Paoletti either for a job or to start a new restaurant in partnership, or know of somebody who'd been approached? Raise your hands."

One hand. Then another. And another. Within moments, two-thirds of the crowd had their hands in the air.

"Nicky was obviously ready to move on," I said to Platt. "You had to be aware of it. You were aware that the Courtyard Café could never be the same without him. No more four-star ratings, that's for certain."

"You're crazy!" shouted Platt. "Nicky was very happy right where he was! He had money, prestige, total control of the menu!"

"When did you find out he wanted to leave?"

"I'm not answering any more of your asinine questions."

"Fine," I said. "I'll ask somebody else. Monique?"

She thought for a moment. "I started hearing rumors about six months ago, like you said."

Platt wailed, "Is *everyone* against me?"

"If you killed Nicky, we are," I said.

His face fell. He flashed a furtive glance at the nearest exit and took a sidling step in that direction. Fitch put a hand on his arm. No way.

"If you couldn't have him, no one could," I said. "Was that it, Roger?"

"You don't understand."

"I understand what happened Wednesday night. You snuck up here and confronted Nicky. You warned him what would happen if he left. And when the warning didn't take, you fed him cyanide."

"It wasn't like that at all—"

"How was it, then?" Fitch challenged.

Platt began to sob. "I pleaded with him to stay. I offered to make him a full partner. I would have gone down on my knees. He *was* the Courtyard Café. Without him, I'd be nothing. Nothing."

He wasn't talking to anyone in particular now, just letting the whole world know. "I couldn't let him get away with it. If he wouldn't cook for me, he couldn't cook for anyone. I poured the poison in his glass and made him drink it. I thought it would be a peaceful death. I really didn't want to hurt him. But he—he—just looked so awful, bucking and twitching on the floor—"

Platt turned to the assembled NAMES members. "I'm not sorry I killed him. He betrayed me." He took a deep breath. "There was still some poison left in the container I'd brought. For a moment I considered taking it myself. Then I saw the bottle of Yquem. That was clever of me, don't you think? To pour the leftover poison in the bottle so everyone would think it was in there all along? No one would know I'd killed poor Nicky, because no one would suspect anyone had tried. They'd just assume someone was trying to kill Poole. Because it's such a common sentiment."

He turned to Fitch. "I suppose I should have taken the poison myself, after all. It doesn't matter, does it? As soon as Nicky left, my restaurant was finished anyway. I might as well be too."

FIFTEEN MINUTES LATER I was outside with Brad Fitch. As we watched a pair of deputies bundling Platt into the backseat of a Santa Barbara County Sheriff's patrol car, I said to the lieutenant, "You were right."

"About what?"

"Remember what you told me a couple of months ago, that day we had lunch at the Belle Terrasse? When we were in the middle of all that Ozzie Cole nonsense?"

"I remember we had lunch. I don't remember what I said."

"You told me that people almost always commit murder for one of two reasons. Love or money."

Fitch nodded. "I wasn't kidding, you know."

"I know. I agreed with you—then and now."

"So what's your point?"

I indicated the departing patrol car. "Platt."

"What about him?"

"Do you think he killed Nicky Paoletti because of money—or because of love?"

Fitch started to reply, then paused for a moment. "I was about to say money, obviously. But now that I think about it, I'm not so sure."

"Maybe both?" I offered.

"Maybe." He chuckled mirthlessly. "There's one for the books. Love *and* money."

"In any case, your theory holds."

"I guess." Fitch rubbed his jaw. "But in the end, what difference does it make? The victim's still dead, isn't he?"

I grunted. "Yeah. He's still dead."

Before the members of NAMES wandered off on their separate ways, Michael Gottberg managed to corral them long enough to poll them and determine that Ted Taylor was indeed in as the newest recruit. It wasn't their normal procedure, but nothing that happened over the past few days could be called normal.

Dad, Poole, and I didn't get out of there until two in the morning. It was nearly three o'clock by the time I got Poole tucked in and managed to stumble to bed myself. I told Poole under no circumstances was he to wake me before 9:00 A.M. If he did, it meant dry Wheaties for breakfast. I'd hold a gun to his head to make sure he choked down every bite.

When the knock came on Sunday morning, awakening me from a dream of ducks nibbling at my toes as if they were turnips, it didn't sound like Poole's rapping. I glanced at the clock: It was 8:50. "Dad?" I said.

"Phone for you, Jack," he said from the other side of the door. "It's Maggie."

I slipped on my pants, opened the door, and padded into

my office. I picked up the phone and said, "Is it really you?"

"Hey, stranger," she said. "Long time no see."

"Tell me about it."

"So?" she said. "Can we get together today, or what? You've been all over the news, you know. Or at least your client has."

"Wait till you get the whole scoop. Tonight."

"Why not sooner?"

"Because I still have to return you-know-who to San Francisco today. I swear I'll be back by this evening. We can have a late supper."

Maggie said that sounded fine and she looked forward to seeing me. We had a lot to catch up on.

On my way back to the guest room, I could hear stirring behind the closed door of my own bedroom. Tonight the room would be mine once again, I thought. Unless I ended up spending the night at Maggie's, in which case I wouldn't be able to move back in till tomorrow. But that would be just fine.

By the time I finished showering, shaving, and dressing, I could hear Poole's and Dad's voices in the kitchen. I hung back, eavsdropping. "Mr. Donne, Mr. Donne," intoned Poole. "Think of the brunch you could serve on weekends. You could even make it a package—a lovely meal followed by a tour of your winery. It could be quite lucrative."

"I'm too old," Dad said. "Maybe you didn't notice, but I don't move around as well as I once did."

"You would have help, of course. Someone to design the menu and supervise the staff. Someone to carry out your orders."

"My staff?"

"Surely."

"How am I supposed to pay them while the business is starting up? And how will I afford the industrial-grade kitchen I'd have to have in order to run a proper restaurant?"

Poole sounded confused. "Is money an issue? Are you short on funds?"

"I wouldn't put it that way, but I certainly don't have the capital to do what you're suggesting."

"Then perhaps I can be of assistance. You have been so generous to me, it would be an honor to repay you in kind. To assist in your search for capital."

"You mean you'd put up the money yourself?"

Poole said quickly, "I? Invest in a restaurant? My good man, I would sooner be restricted to a diet of nothing but Big Macs and diet cola than invest in such a trauma-inducing enterprise. I was merely suggesting that I could introduce you to some people with disposable funds."

Dad said, "I think I'll just stick with the winery."

Thank you, I whispered to myself.

WE DROVE TO Bakersfield in the Cadillac and caught a northbound train back to the Bay Area. Poole spent the whole trip recounting and embellishing our adventures of the past days. I listened, nodded agreement at the appropriate times, and tried not to doze off.

We caught a cab at the Emeryville station. When we got to Jones Street, I told the cabbie to wait. Following Poole's directions, I dragged his luggage into the house, then up his private elevator to his bedroom, where I dumped off the bags.

He'd promised to wait for me in his office. He was at his place behind the massive desk, a leather-bound checkbook open in front of him. He'd written the check and was signing with a flourish. "Here is your fee," he said. "Four thousand, five hundred dollars for five days of service at nine hundred dollars a day.

You can send me the bill for the damage done to your vehicle. I've also included a five-hundred-dollar bonus."

"What for?" I asked.

"For having shown me as splendid a time as I've had in my life."

I thanked him, took the check, folded it, and placed it in my pocket. He let out a small laugh. "At first I was afraid I mightn't be able to pay you. I didn't know where Miss Lubow kept my checkbook."

"I'm glad you found it." I gave him a little wave of farewell. "So long, Mr. Poole. I've got a cab waiting outside, and—"

"I dismissed it."

"Come again?"

"The cab. I dismissed it. We have some—other business to discuss."

"What other business?"

He sighed. "It really is going to be difficult for me, having to carry on without Miss Lubow."

"I'm sure you'll find someone."

"It is of the utmost importance to me that I replace her immediately." A pause. "How would you like the position, Mr. Donne?"

"Me?"

"Certainly. You are intelligent, resourceful, loyal. You are familiar with the circles in which I travel. It would be an ideal match."

"It would be a lousy match."

He waved a hand. "I know, I know. The job would lack the excitement that you are accustomed to. That is why, before you make your decision, you should allow me to complete the proposition."

"What proposition?"

"I've decided to go into the private detective business."

I stood there gaping at him, trying to make up my mind if this was some bizarre joke or simply evidence he'd gone off the deep end. "I consider myself well suited to the trade," Poole went on. "Having absolutely no prior experience, I solved the murder of Niccolo Paoletti when an entire police force could not. Your assistance made that task infinitely simpler, of course. Mr. Donne, I would like you to come to work for me as both my personal assistant and my business associate. What do you say?"

"What do I say?" I stepped up close to him and looked him in the eye. "Mr. Poole, I'd rather be dragged across the Mojave Desert by my tongue than work for you—much less with you— ever again. Good-bye and good luck."

With that, I took his hand and gave it a hearty shake. He was too amazed to pull away from the unexpected contact. Then I marched out of the office, pulled open the front door, stepped outside, and ambled down the street to track down another taxi. All the while whistling happily.